THE FIRST ARMADA GHOST BOOK

CONTENTS

INTRODUCTION

There is a big difference between *being* frightened—and actually *choosing* to be frightened. The pleasures of fear have been described as 'being frightened *in a safe place*". I can only say that that never worked for me. I recall reading Edgar Allan Poe in bed, the gas fire popping, the curtains drawn against the winter weather . . . and the sudden paralysis of fear, restricting breathing, spreading slowly but surely to toes and finger tips, caused by a total inability to turn over and find what beastliness lay on the next page! Would it get better or worse? What, if you please, lurked in the coffin? (Nothing as restful as a quiet dead body, that was for sure.) What agency screamed in the long gallery? . . . *and why were my curtains moving*? Never-to-be-forgotten, delicious torment. . . .

So I can only warn those of you who don't like being frightened that some of these stories are pretty scary and can only be read by people who actually enjoy experiencing a sudden shock, the cold hand of fear. *The Red Room, School for the Unspeakable* and *The House of the Nightmare* are three I rate high in shock value. *School for the Unspeakable* plumbs the depths of misery which, only a couple of generations ago, some unlucky people had to survive at those dreadful, Dickensian boarding schools. The ghastly experiences of poor Bart Setwick, that "honest-faced, well-knit lad in tweeds" are appallingly vivid.

Some stories, in spite of many gruesome ingredients, fail to print themselves on the memory. But *The House of the Nightmare* has, I think, a fine feeling for atmosphere

The First Armada
Ghost Book

EDITED BY
CHRISTINE BERNARD

COVER BY
PETER ARCHER

ILLUSTRATED BY
GINO D'ACHILLE

Armada

The arrangement of this
Collection is copyright

© CHRISTINE BERNARD 1967

The *First Armada Ghost Book* was first
published in the U.K. in 1967 by May Fair
Books Ltd., 14 St. James's Place, London
S.W.1, and was printed in Great Britain by
Love & Malcomson Ltd., Brighton Road,
Redhill, Surrey.

and place. The strange manner in which it begins, the sense of unreality that I—and perhaps you—have experienced cycling along between unfamiliar fields and woods . . . in spite of its sadness the story leaves one with a feeling of unearthly beauty that lingers long after it is finished. As to *The Red Room*, it could be described as the ultimate in ghost stories because no one wastes time rattling chains, moaning, or thumping around in the middle of the night; it is in fact, all about, and only about, fear itself.

Whether we like it or not, it is natural to laugh at the misfortunes of others—and I have never seen why ghosts shouldn't be funny too. That is why I have included humour in this collection. I laughed a great deal at the misfortunes of *The Water Ghost of Harrowby Hall* who had a harsh time of it when she was finally ousted. After all, she had been a dreadful nuisance for hundreds of years! *The Inexperienced Ghost* made a remarkable mess of things, both as a human *and* as a ghost. Both of them illustrate the theory that, failure apart, dignity is a precarious business. They would have done well to remember the old saws: know the size of your enemy—and never bite off more than you can chew—particularly when, like the Inexperienced Ghost, you are considering a new profession. If, for instance, *you* feel like taking up the haunting game do make sure you are properly equipped. There is absolutely nothing more degrading than arranging a series of nerve-racking squeals, clankings and groanings only to have someone say, "Heavens, I really must get that door oiled. . . ."

Scotland, often the source of marvellously macabre tales, is well represented in this collection. I chose them partly because their humour appealed to me, and also because they are very convincing. Their author, Sorche Nic Leodhas, has written: "Ghost stories are among my earliest memories for I am an attracter of ghost-story-tellers. I cannot even remember when people started to seek me out with news of the supernatural world. *And they all believe that what they are telling me is true.*"

Children have always figured in ghostly accounts, both real and imaginary. Students of the supernatural say they have a special sensory gift which brings them closer to the unknown—that their minds, as yet uncluttered with the paraphernalia of adulthood, are more open to unseen influences. . . . Perhaps that is why children are so often central characters in famous stories like *The House of the Nightmare, Spooks of the Valley*—and that delightful one, *A Pair of Hands*, the heroine of which is surely the nicest, gentlest little ghost one could hope to meet.

So here are tales for your amusement and discomfort, your pleasure and haunting . . . all of which might please some of you, and some of which, I very much hope, will please all of you. Good, nervous, reading to you!

CHRISTINE BERNARD

SANDY MacNEIL AND HIS DOG

By Sorche Nic Leodhas

THERE ONCE was a man named Sandy NacNeil who lived just outside Cairncraigie. His family in the old days had had plenty of lands and money, but that was in his great-grandsire's time. Then the troubled times came along, and when they were over, his great grandsire was gone and all the gold and gear had got themselves lost somehow, too. So all that was handed down to Sandy were a few starve-crow fields and an old tumble-down house.

Sandy was never one to mourn for what was gone and long gone. He made do with what he had and managed to scrape by on it. Being an easy-going, good-natured sort of a lad, he wasted no time complaining, and as he went his own gait and let his neighbours do the same he had plenty of friends and no enemies worth mentioning. All in all, he was as happy-go-lucky and contented as if he'd been a laird.

There was one queer thing about Sandy MacNeil. He had a terrible fancy for dogs, and they had the same for him. He'd be coming down to the village of a Saturday night, and every tyke in the place would prick up its ears and wag its tail as he passed by. Sandy'd go along to the tavern to have a friendly gab about the news of the week with whoever dropped in, and by the time he got there, a dozen or maybe more dogs would be footing it along before and behind him. Each one of them would be trying to shoulder the next one away to get closer to Sandy, and him talking away to them all the while. 'Twas a rare comical thing to see!

When Sandy came to the tavern door, he'd stop, and all the dogs would stop, too. Then Sandy would say polite-like, "That's all for now, laddies. Be off to your homes, for I cannot ask you in with me."

Then the dogs would wag their tails to show there was no offence taken, and off they'd go back to their homes, just as Sandy told them to do.

Some folks remarked that it was a queer thing that Sandy MacNeil had no dog of his own. But others would say, why should he, when every other man's dog was just as much his as its master's. Still, the time came when Sandy did get a dog for himself, though the getting of it was no doing of his own.

This is the way it all came about.

One night Sandy was coming home from Cairncraigie. It was past nightfall, for he'd stayed longer than he meant to, the company being good and the talk entertaining. He was swinging along at a fair rate, because the morrow was the Sabbath, and there were jobs that had to be done before midnight came so that he'd not be working on a Sunday.

It was a misty, cloudy sort of a night with a pale moon overhead that gave little light, being mostly behind a cloud. Besides, the road was dark because on either side there were tall hedges that cast their shadows on it. Maybe that's why Sandy didn't notice the dog. He did think once or twice that something was there, but he put it down to a fox or maybe a badger. Being in haste to get home, he paid it no heed.

It wasn't till he got to the place where the road met his own lane that he saw it. The hedge stopped there to let the lane through to the road. Just as Sandy got there the moon came peeping out for a minute from under the clouds. That was when he first caught sight of the dog.

Sandy had never seen its like before. The creature looked to be the size of a young calf, and it had long legs and a rough, shaggy coat of fur. From the point of its muzzle to the tip of its tail it was black as coal. The moon went back behind the clouds then, so that was all that Sandy saw of it for the time. But the dog must have had its head turned towards Sandy, because he could see its eyes. The eyes shone with a bright red glow that made Sandy think of the way embers glow under the dead coals when a fire is about to go out.

Sandy was acquainted with all the dogs for miles around, and even from the little he'd seen of this dog he knew that it wasn't one of them. He never thought of being afraid, for he had yet to see the creature that could give him a fright. So he called the dog to come to him. The dog never made a move or a sound. It just stood there with those shining red eyes fixed on Sandy.

"Please yourself!" said Sandy, and he turned into the lane towards his house.

The dog came along with him, keeping to its own side of the road and well away from Sandy. It was plain to see that it had no wish to be friendly. Sandy had great respect for the rights of dogs, as well as of men, so he let it be.

When Sandy got up to his house, the dog was still there. "Now, lad," said Sandy. "'Tis sure you've come a long way from your home; for if you lived near I'd be knowing you. By that same token, you've a long journey to go before you get home again. You'd best be off and away!'"

But the minute Sandy opened the door the dog slipped by him into the house.

"Och now!" cried Sandy. "Come out o' there, my lad! Where'er you belong, 'tis not here."

But the dog did not come out and, what with the house so dark and the dog so black, Sandy couldn't see where it was at all.

Sandy went in and found a lamp. He lit it, and then he looked about for the dog. He found it lying on the bench by the fire in the front room. It lay with its nose down on its paws, and its eyes gleaming at Sandy with the same red glow. Now that Sandy could look at it by lamplight, he could see what a huge creature it was. He'd vow it was twice the size of any he'd e'er seen before. But it wasn't its uncommon size that gave Sandy a queer sort of feeling, but something else about it that Sandy couldn't put into words.

However, dogs were dogs, and Sandy was fond of them all. So he said, "Well then, lie there. Rest yourself a bit if you like. Happen you're weary, poor creature."

Sandy went about getting things ready for the morn. When he'd finished and filled the kettle and laid out his Sunday clothes, he said coaxingly, "Come away now,

12

black laddie! 'Tis time for you to be off to where you belong."

He opened the house door for the dog to go out. The dog made no move to go, but lay still upon the bench. Sandy was used to having dogs do what he told them to do, and it surprised him that this one didn't mind him.

"Happen he's deaf!" he told himself. So he went over to the dog to give it a nudge off the bench. He laid his hand on the dog's shoulder. There was no feeling of flesh or fur under his hand and his fingers came down flat on the bench!

Sandy snatched his hand away as if he'd burnt it. A shiver ran up his spine and back down again. Then he laughed at himself. Half asleep on his feet he must be, and dreaming! It was late and he must be more tired than he'd thought. He went and took the lamp up from the table, carried it over to the fire, and leaned over the bench to take a good look at the dog. He nearly dropped the lamp! He wasn't dreaming! Losh! 'Twas no proper dog there at all! *'Twas the ghost of a dog!*

Sandy backed away. He set the lamp down on the table, his fingers trembling so that it was all he could do to put it upright. Then he sat down to think it over. Of one thing he was sure. He'd not tamper with the creature any further. So the dog lay and looked at Sandy, and Sandy looked at the dog.

What the dog was thinking about a body couldn't tell. At first, Sandy couldn't think at all, but after a while his wits came back to him, and he started to reason the matter out. Ghost or not, the dog appeared to mean him no harm. Sandy told himself that if he were going to be haunted at all, he'd rather be haunted by the ghost of a dog than many another he could think of. His great-grandsire, for one, who'd have made a raring ranting old bogle from all that Sandy'd ever heard tell of him. Anyhow, the ghost was there and meant to stay, so what could Sandy do about it? Having come to this conclusion, Sandy told himself that a man needed his rest. So he blew out the lamp and went to bed. And after a while he got off to sleep.

When he woke in the morn he laughed to himself. "Och!" he said. "That was a rare fine dream I was having the night's night." And he went yawning down the stairs to put the kettle over the fire for his morning tea. He looked over at the bench as he passed by the front-room door, just sort of making sure it was a dream.

The dog was still there!

Then and there Sandy made up his mind.

"If I can't drive you out," he said to the dog, "neither shall you drive me out. 'Tis my house and I'm staying in it. The place is big enough for the two of us."

So the dog stayed with Sandy, and Sandy stayed with the dog. At first, Sandy had an eerie feeling seeing it lying there as he came in and out of the house, knowing what it was. But that soon wore off, and he paid it no heed at all. To tell the truth, after a week or two he began to like having it there. It was company for him, living alone as he did.

Except for the night he met it on the road, Sandy never saw it anywhere but on the bench by the fire,

14

although sometimes, as he came up the lane, he had a fancy that it was walking beside him. But when he came into the house, it was always there on the bench.

Sandy never told folk he had a dog, but it wasn't long till they found out for themselves. They found out what sort of a dog it was, too.

One evening, a neighbour of Sandy's stopped by to ask for the loan of some tool or other, and when Sandy stepped out of the house to give it to him, he left the door standing open.

While Sandy stood on the doorstep talking to him, the man—being the sort that is always curious about other folk—peered into the room. He saw the great black dog lying on the bench by the fire.

"Och then!" said the man. "You've got yourself a dog at last, Sandy MacNeil."

"Happen I have," Sandy said.

"'Tis an odd-looking creature!" the man exclaimed, leaning to look past Sandy.

"Happen it is," said Sandy, and he reached behind himself to pull the door to.

The neighbour had a lot more curiosity than he had wits. "I'll just have a look at it then," he said, pushing past Sandy into the room.

"I'd not advise it," Sandy warned him. But the man was already across the room and had his hand on the dog.

The haste with which the man left Sandy's house was amazing. He screeched something at Sandy as he flew past, but what it was Sandy could never tell. Before Sandy could tell him the dog would do him no harm, he was out of sight.

15

To be sure, the news spread like fire in dry corn stubble. Soon there wasn't anybody that didn't know that Sandy had got a dog for himself that was the ghost of a dog.

It nearly turned the village upside down. Some folk said nothing at all and some said they'd not go near Sandy MacNeil's house for love nor money. But there was an awful sluagh of folk that took it upon themselves to give Sandy a word of advice.

Sandy was used to going his own gait and didn't like being interfered with, so he gave this lot the rough edge of his tongue.

"'Tis no concern of yours what kind of dog I've got," he said angrily.

"Ye'd do well to get rid of it," they insisted.

"Get rid of it!" Sandy said hotly. "Och, why should I do that?"

"'Tis unnatural, a dog's ghaist," they said.

"It does no harm," Sandy insisted.

"Not yet," said they.

"Nor ever will," retorted Sandy. "He suits me fine! Not a penny does he cost me, for he doesn't need to be fed or tended. Nor does he keep folk awake o' nights baying at the moon like the tykes of some folk I could be naming. He can bide with me as long as he likes, so hauld your whisht!"

The truth was that, ghost or no ghost, the dog was Sandy's dog and he'd got terribly fond of it.

What he minded most was that folk wouldn't stop havering about it. It was all they talked about at the tavern and a man could find no comfort there any more. It was just as bad when they met him on the

16

road or in the village. Nobody could find anything to talk about but the big black dog that was a ghost and that was going to bring Sandy terrible bad luck.

One Saturday evening he came home from the village and sat down to take off his boots by the fire. He'd come away extra early, because he couldn't see any sense in staying there because of the way they all kept on at him.

He looked over to the dog and said to it, "If it's any sort o' luck you're going to bring me, be at it and let's have done with it! Either that or do something to stop their blethering, for I'm weary of hearing them go on about it."

And being so put out and upset by it all, he did what he'd never have done to a dog had he not been driven to it. He took the boot he had in his hand and hurled it at the dog.

The boot never went near the dog, for which Sandy was glad, because he'd never meant to throw it.

"Och, lad!" said he to the dog. "'Tis sorry I am!"

But the dog looked at him for a minute with its eyes glowing redder than ever, and then it leapt down from the bench and up the stairs. Sandy ran after to see what it was up to, but the dog had too much of a start on him. Just as Sandy got to the top of the stairs the dog gave a great bound that took it right through the wall. Where it went through, it left behind a great hole in the wall, and Sandy ran over to see if he could find out where the dog had gone.

When Sandy got to the hole, he found that it wasn't a hole at all. Instead it was a hidden cupboard that he had never known was there, because it was behind the

Out poured a great stream of golden coins

plaster that had long ago been laid over it. The door of the cupboard stood open now, and while Sandy stood and stared at it a great bag fell off the shelf and dinged down on the floor. The bag flew open, and out poured a great stream of golden coins.

Sandy fell on to his knees before it. "Luck!" he cried. "Och, here's all the luck in the world! And 'twas my big black dog that brought it to me!"

It was his great-grandsire's gold that had got itself lost, because he had hidden it away there before he went off to fight in the troubled times. Since he'd got himself killed, he never came back to tell them where it was.

Sandy gathered the gold up into a basket and took it down to the village to show folk the kind of luck the ghost of the big black dog had brought him. The ones who had the most to say before were the very ones who had the least to say when they saw the gold.

The sorry thing for Sandy was that he never saw the dog again, and he missed it sorely. He waited long for it to come back, and there were times he told himself he'd rather have it than all his great-grandsire's gold. But at last he gave up waiting and got himself a tyke to keep him company. It wasn't as big or black or quiet as the other, but it helped.

Now that Sandy was the richest man in the countryside, folk took to calling him The MacNeil, to show their respect. He found himself a bonnie young wife and built himself a fine new house, which he called "Dog's Luck" just to remind folk where his money came from.

He still goes into the village of a Saturday night, and

if you should be there and see a man with a dozen or
more dogs footing it along before and behind him, each
trying to shoulder the next one out of the way to get
closer to him, you'll know that's Sandy MacNeil.

SCHOOL FOR THE UNSPEAKABLE

By MANLY WADE WELLMAN

BART SETWICK dropped off the train at Carrington and
stood for a moment on the station platform, an honest-
faced, well-knit lad in tweeds. This little town and its
famous school would be his home for the next eight
months; but which way to the school? The sun had set,
and he could barely see the shop signs across
Carrington's modest main street. He hesitated, and a
soft voice spoke at his very elbow:

"Are you for the school?"

Startled, Bart Setwick wheeled. In the grey twilight
stood another youth, smiling thinly and waiting as if
for an answer. The stranger was all of nineteen years
old—that meant maturity to young Setwick, who was
fifteen—and his pale face had shrewd lines to it. His
tall, shambling body was clad in high-necked jersey
and unfashionably tight trousers. Bart Setwick
skimmed him with the quick, appraising eye of young
America.

"I just got here," he replied. "My name's Setwick."

"Mine's Hoag." Out came a slender hand. Setwick took it and found it froggy-cold, with a suggestion of steel-wire muscles. "Glad to meet you. I came down on the chance someone would drop off the train. Let me give you a lift to the school."

Hoak turned away, felinely light for all his ungainliness, and led his new acquaintance around the corner of the little wooden railway station. Behind the structure, half hidden in its shadow, stood a shabby buggy with a lean bay horse in the shafts.

"Get in," invited Hoag, but Bart Setwick paused for a moment. His generation was not used to such vehicles. Hoag chuckled and said, "Oh, this is only a school wrinkle. We run to funny customs. Get in."

Setwick obeyed. "How about my trunk?"

"Leave it." The taller youth swung himself in beside Setwick and took the reins. "You'll not need it tonight."

He snapped his tongue and the bay horse stirred, drew them around and off down a bush-lined road. Its hoofbeats were oddly muffled.

They turned a corner, another, and came into open country. The lights of Carrington, newly kindled against the night, hung behind like a constellation settled down to Earth. Setwick felt a hint of chill that did not seem to fit the September evening.

"How far is the school from town?" he asked.

"Four or five miles," Hoag replied in his hushed voice. "That was deliberate on the part of the founders —they wanted to make it hard for the students to get to town for larks. It forced us to dig up our own amusements." The pale face creased in a faint smile, as

21

if this were a pleasantry. "There's just a few of the right sort on hand tonight. By the way, what did you get sent out for?"

Setwick frowned his mystification. "Why, to go to school. Dad sent me."

"But what for? Don't you know that this is a high-class prison prep? Half of us are lunkheads that need poking along, the other half are fellows who got in scandals somewhere else. Like me." Again Hoag smiled.

Setwick began to dislike his companion. They rolled a mile or so in silence before Hoag again asked a question:

"Do you go to church, Setwick?"

The new boy was afraid to appear priggish, and made a careless show with, "Not very often."

"Can you recite anything from the Bible," Hoag's soft voice took on an anxious tinge.

"Not that I know of."

"Good," was the almost hearty response. "As I was saying, there's only a few of us at the school tonight— only three, to be exact. And we don't like Bible-quoters."

Setwick laughed, trying to appear sage and cynical. "Isn't Satan reputed to quote the Bible to his own——"

"What do you know about Satan?" interrupted Hoag. He turned full on Setwick, studying him with intent, dark eyes. Then, as if answering his own question: "Little enough, I'll bet. Would you like to know about him?"

22

"Sure I would," replied Setwick, wondering what the joke would be.

"I'll teach you after a while," Hoag promised cryptically, and silence fell again.

Half a moon was well up as they came in sight of a dark jumble of buildings.

"Here we are," announced Hoag, and then, throwing back his head, he emitted a wild, wordless howl that made Setwick almost jump out of the buggy. "That's to let the others know we're coming," he explained. "Listen!"

Back came a seeming echo of the howl, shrill, faint and eerie. The horse wavered in its muffled trot, and Hoag clucked it back into step. They turned in at a driveway well grown up in weeds, and two minutes more brought them up to the rear of the closest building. It was dim grey in the wash of moonbeams, with blank inky rectangles for windows. Nowhere was there a light, but as the buggy came to a halt Setwick saw a young head pop out of a window on the lower floor.

"Here already, Hoag?" came a high, reedy voice.

"Yes," answered the youth at the reins, "and I've brought a new man with me."

Thrilling a bit to hear himself called a man, Setwick alighted.

"His name's Setwick," went on Hoag. "Meet Andoff, Setwick. A great friend of mine."

Andoff flourished a hand in greeting and scrambled out over the window-sill. He was chubby and squat and even paler than Hoag, with a low forehead beneath

23

lank, wet-looking hair, and black eyes set wide apart in a fat, stupid-looking face. His shabby jacket was too tight for him, and beneath worn knickers his legs and feet were bare. He might have been an overgrown thirteen or an undeveloped eighteen.

"Felcher ought to be along in half a second," he volunteered.

"Entertain Setwick while I put up the buggy," Hoag directed him.

Andoff nodded, and Hoag gathered the lines in his hands, but paused for a final word.

"No funny business yet, Andoff," he cautioned seriously. "Setwick, don't let this lard-bladder rag you or tell you wild stories until I come back."

Andoff laughed shrilly. "No, no wild stories," he promised. "You'll do the talking, Hoag."

The buggy trundled away, and Andoff swung his fat, grinning face to the new arrival.

"Here comes Felcher," he announced. "Felcher, meet Setwick."

Another boy had bobbed up, it seemed, from nowhere. Setwick had not seen him come around the corner of the building, or slip out of a door or window. He was probably as old as Hoag, or older, but so small as to be almost a dwarf, and frail to boot. His most notable characteristic was his hairiness. A great mop covered his head, brushed over his neck and ears, and hung unkemptly to his bright, deepset eyes. His lips and cheeks were spread with a rank down, and a curly thatch peeped through the unbuttoned collar of his soiled white shirt. The hand he offered Setwick was almost simian in its shagginess and in the hardness of its palm. Too, it was cold and damp. Setwick remembered the same thing of Hoag's handclasp.

"We're the only ones here so far." Felcher remarked. His voice, surprisingly deep and strong for so small a creature, rang like a great bell.

"Isn't even the headmaster here?" inquired Setwick, and at that the other two began to laugh uproariously, Andoff's fife-squeal rendering an obligato to Felcher's bell-boom. Hoag, returning, asked what the fun was.

"Setwick asks," groaned Felcher, "why the headmaster isn't here to welcome him."

More fife-laughter and bell-laughter.

"I doubt if Setwick would think the answer was funny," Hoag commented, and then chuckled softly himself.

Setwick, who had been well brought up, began to grow nettled.

"Tell me about it," he urged, in what he hoped was a bleak tone, "and I'll join your chorus of mirth."

Felcher and Andoff gazed at him with eyes strangely eager and learning. Then they faced Hoag.

"Let's tell him," they both said at once, but Hoag shook his head.

"Not yet. One thing at a time. Let's have the song first."

They began to sing. The first verse of their offering was obscene, with no pretense of humour to redeem it. Setwick had never been squeamish, but he found himself definitely repelled. The second verse seemed less objectionable, but it hardly made sense:

All they tried to teach here
Now goes untaught.
Ready, steady, each here,
Knowledge we sought.
What they called disaster
Killed us not, O master!
Rule us, we beseech here,
Eye, hand and thought.

It was something like a hymn, Setwick decided; but before what altar would such hymns be sung? Hoag must have read that question in his mind.

"You mentioned Satan in the buggy on the way out," he recalled, his knowing face hanging like a mask in the half-dimness close to Setwick. "Well, that was a Satanist song."

"It was? Who made it?"

"I did," Hoag informed him. "How do you like it?"

Setwick made no answer. He tried to sense mockery in Hoag's voice, but could not find it. "What," he asked finally, "does all this Satanist singing have to do with the headmaster?"

"A lot," came back Felcher deeply, and "A lot," squealed Andoff.

Hoag gazed from one of his friends to the others, and for the first time he smiled broadly. It gave him a toothy look.

"I believe," he ventured quietly but weightily, "that we might as well let Setwick in on the secret of our little circle."

Here it would begin, the new boy decided—the school hazing of which he had heard and read so much.

He had anticipated such things with something of excitement, even eagerness, but now he wanted none of them. He did not like his three companions, and he did not like the way they approached whatever it was they intended to do. He moved backward a pace or two, as if to retreat.

Swift as darting birds, Hoag and Andoff closed in at either elbow. Their chill hands clutched him and suddenly he felt light-headed and sick. Things that had been clear in the moonlight went hazy and distorted.

"Come on and sit down, Setwick," invited Hoag, as though from a great distance. His voice did not grow loud or harsh, but it embodied real menace. "Sit on that window-sill. Or would you like us to carry you?"

At the moment Setwick wanted only to be free of their touch, and so he walked unresistingly to the sill and scrambled up on it. Behind him was the blackness of an unknown chamber, and at his knees gathered the three who seemed so eager to tell him their private joke.

"The headmaster was a proper churchgoer," began Hoag, as though he were the spokesman for the group. "He didn't have any use for devils or devil-worship. Went on record against them when he addressed us in chapel. That was what started us."

"Right," nodded Andoff, turning up his fat, larval face. "Anything he outlawed, we wanted to do. Isn't that logic?"

"Logic and reason," wound up Felcher. His hairy right hand twiddled on the sill near Setwick's thigh. In the moonlight it looked like a big, nervous spider.

27

Hoag resumed. "I don't know of any prohibition of his it was easier or more fun to break."

Setwick found that his mouth had gone dry. His tongue could barely moisten his lips. "You mean," he said, "that you began to worship devils?"

Hoag nodded happily, like a teacher at an apt pupil. "One vacation I got a book on the cult. The three of us studied it, then began ceremonies. We learned the charms and spells, forward and backward——"

"They're twice as good backward," put in Felcher, and Andoff giggled.

"Have you any idea, Setwick." Hoag almost cooed, "what it was that appeared in our study the first time we burned wine and sulphur, with the proper words spoken over them?"

Setwick did not want to know. He clenched his teeth. "If you're trying to scare me," he managed to growl out, "it certainly isn't going to work."

All three laughed once more, and began to chatter out their protestations of good faith.

"I swear that we're telling the truth, Setwick." Hoag assured him. "Do you want to hear it, or don't you?"

Setwick had very little choice in the matter, and he realised it. "Oh, go ahead," he capitulated, wondering how it would do to crawl backward from the sill into the darkness of the room.

Hoag, leaned toward him, with the air as of one confiding. "The headmaster caught us. Caught us red-handed."

"Book open, fire burning," chanted Felcher.

"He had something very fine to say about the vengeance of heaven," Hoag went on. "We got to laughing at him. He worked up a frenzy. Finally he tried to take heaven's vengeance into his own hands—tried to visit it on us, in a very primitive way. But it didn't work."

Andoff was laughing immoderately, his fat arms across his bent belly.

"He thought it worked," he supplemented between high gurgles, "but it didn't."

"Nobody could kill us," Felcher added. "Not after the oaths we'd taken, and the promises that had been made us."

"What promises?" demanded Setwick, who was struggling hard not to believe. "Who made you any promises?"

"Those we worshipped," Felcher told him. If he was simulating earnestness, it was a supreme bit of acting. Setwick, realising this, was more daunted than he cared to show.

"When did all these things happen?" was his next question.

"When?" echoed Hoag. "Oh, years and years ago."

"Years and years ago," repeated Andoff.

"Long before you were born," Felcher assured him.

They were standing close together, their backs to the moon that shone in Setwick's face. He could not see their expressions clearly. But their three voices—Hoag's soft, Felcher's deep and vibrant, Andoff's high and squeaky—were absolutely serious.

"I know what you're arguing within yourself," Hoag announced somewhat smugly. "How can we, who talk about those many past years, seem so young? That calls for an explanation, I'll admit." He paused, as if choosing words. "Time—for us—stands still. It came to a halt on that very night, Setwick; the night our headmaster tried to put an end to our worship."

"And to us," smirked the gross-bodied Andoff, with his usual air of self-congratulation at capping one of Hoag's statements.

"The worship goes on," pronounced Felcher, in the same chanting manner that he had affected once before. "The worship goes on, and we go on, too."

"Which brings us to the point," Hoag came in briskly. "Do you want to throw in with us, Setwick?— make the fourth of this lively little party?"

"No, I don't," snapped Setwick vehemently.

They fell silent, and gave back a little—a trio of bizarre silhouettes against the pale moonglow. Setwick could see the flash of their staring eyes among the shadows of their faces. He knew that he was afraid, but hid his fear. Pluckily he dropped from the sill to the ground. Dew from the grass spattered his sock-clad ankles between oxfords and trouser-cuffs.

"I guess it's my turn to talk," he told them levelly. "I'll make it short. I don't like you, nor anything you've said. And I'm getting out of here."

"We won't let you," said Hoag, hushed but emphatic.

"We won't let you," murmured Andoff and Felcher together, as though they had rehearsed it a thousand times.

Setwick clenched his fists. His father had taught him to box. He took a quick, smooth stride toward Hoag and hit him hard in the face. Next moment all three had flung themselves upon him. They did not seem to strike or grapple or tug, but he went down under their assault. The shoulders of his tweed coat wallowed in sand, and he smelled crushed weeds. Hoag, on top of him, pinioned his arms with a knee on each bicep. Felcher and Andoff were stooping close.

Glaring up in helpless rage, Setwick knew once and for all that this was no schoolboy prank Never did practical jokers gather around their victim with such staring, green-gleaming eyes, such drawn jowls, such quivering lips.

Hoag bared white fangs. His pointed tongue quested once over them.

"Knife!" he muttered, and Felcher fumbled in a pocket, then passed him something that sparkled in the moonlight.

Hoag's lean hand reached for it, then whipped back. Hoag had lifted his eyes to something beyond the huddle. He choked and whimpered inarticulately, sprang up from Setwick's labouring chest. and fell back in awkward haste. The others followed his shocked stare, then as suddenly cowered and retreated in turn.

"It's the master!" wailed Andoff.

"Yes," roared a gruff new voice. "Your old headmaster—and I've come back to master *you!*"

Rising upon one elbow, the prostrate Setwick saw what they had seen—a tall, thick-bodied figure in a long dark coat, topped with a square, distorted face and a tousle of white locks. Its eyes glittered with their own pale, hard light. As it advanced slowly and heavily it emitted a snigger of murderous joy. Even at first glance Setwick was aware that it cast no shadow.

31

"I am in time," mouthed the newcomer. "You were going to kill this poor boy."

Hoag had recovered and made a stand. "Kill him?" he quavered, seeming to fawn before the threatening presence. "No. We'd have given him life——"

"You call it life!" trumpeted the long-coated one. "You'd have sucked out his blood to teem your own dead veins, damned him to your filthy condition. But I'm here to prevent you!"

A finger pointed, huge and knuckly, and then came a torrent of language. To the nerve-stunned Setwick it sounded like a bit from the New Testament, or perhaps from the Book of Common Prayer. All at once he remembered Hoag's avowed dislike for such quotations.

His three erstwhile assailants reeled as if before a high wind that chilled or scorched. "No, no! Don't!" they begged wretchedly.

The square old face gaped open and spewed merciless laughter. The knuckly finger traced a cross in the air, and the trio wailed in chorus as though the sign had been drawn upon their flesh with a tongue of flame.

Hoag dropped to his knees. "Don't!" he sobbed.

"I have power," mocked their tormentor. "During years shut up I won it, and now I'll use it." Again a triumphant burst of mirth. "I know you're damned and can't be killed, but you can be tortured! I'll make you crawl like worms before I'm done with you!"

Setwick gained his shaky feet. The long coat and the blocky head leaned toward him.

"Run, you!" dinned a rough roar in his ears. "Get out of here—and thank God for the chance!"

Setwick ran, staggering. He blundered through the weeds of the driveway, gained the road beyond. In the distance gleamed the lights of Carrington. As he turned his face toward them and quickened his pace he began to weep, chokingly, hysterically, exhaustingly.

He did not stop running until he reached the platform in front of the station. A clock across the street struck ten, in a deep voice not unlike Felcher's. Setwick breathed deeply, fished out his handkerchief and mopped his face. His hand was quivering like a grass stalk in a breeze.

"Beg pardon!" came a cheery hail. "You must be Setwick."

As once before on this same platform, he whirled around with startled speed. Within touch of him stood a broad-shouldered man of thirty or so, with horn-rimmed spectacles. He wore a neat Norfolk jacket and flannels. A short briar pipe was clamped in a good-humoured mouth.

"I'm Collins, one of the masters at the school," he introduced himself. "If you're Setwick, you've had us worried. We expected you on that seven o'clock train, you know. I dropped down to see if I couldn't trace you."

Setwick found a little of his lost wind. "But I've—been to the school," he mumbled protestingly. His hand, still trembling, gestured vaguely along the way he had come.

Collins threw back his head and laughed, then apologised.

33

"Sorry," he said. "It's no joke if you really had all that walk for nothing. Why, that old place is deserted —used to be a catch-all for incorrigible rich boys. They closed it about fifty years ago, when the headmaster went mad and killed three of his pupils. As a matter of coincidence, the master himself died just this afternoon, in the state hospital for the insane."

THE HOUSE OF THE NIGHTMARE

By Edward Lucas White

I FIRST caught sight of the house from the brow of the mountain as I cleared the woods and looked across the broad valley several hundred feet below me, to the low sun sinking toward the far blue hills. From that momentary viewpoint I had an exaggerated sense of looking almost vertically down. I seemed to be hanging over the chequer-board of roads and fields, dotted with farm buildings, and felt the familiar deception that I could almost throw a stone upon the house. I barely glimpsed its slate roof.

What caught my eyes was the bit of road in front of it, between the mass of dark-green trees about the house and the orchard opposite. Perfectly straight it was, bordered by an even row of trees, through which I made out a cinder side path and a low stone wall.

Conspicuous on the orchard side between two of the

flanking trees was a white object, which I took to be a tall stone, a vertical splinter of one of the tilted limestone reefs with which the fields of the region are scarred.

The road itself I saw plain as a boxwood ruler on a green baize table. It gave me a pleasurable anticipation of a chance for a burst of speed. I had been painfully traversing closely forested, semi-mountainous hills. Not a farmhouse had I passed, only wretched cabins by the road, more than twenty miles of which I had found very bad and hindering. Now, when I was not many miles from my expected stopping-place, I looked forward to better going, and to that straight, level bit in particular.

As I sped cautiously down the sharp beginning of the long descent the trees engulfed me again, and I lost sight of the valley. I dipped into a hollow, rose on the crest of the new hill, and again saw the house, nearer, and not so far below.

The tall stone caught my eye with a shock of surprise. Had I not thought it was opposite the house next the orchard? Clearly it was on the left-hand side of the road toward the house. My self-questioning lasted only the moment as I passed the crest. Then the outlook was cut off again; but I found myself gazing ahead, watching for the next chance at the same view.

At the end of the second hill I only saw the bit of road obliquely and could not be sure, but, as at first, the tall stone seemed on the right of the road.

At the top of the third and last hill I looked down the stretch of road under the over-arching trees, almost as one would look through a tube. There was a line of whiteness which I took for the tall stone. It was on the right.

I dipped into the last hollow. As I mounted the farther slope I kept my eyes on the top of the road ahead of me. When my line of sight surmounted the rise I marked the tall stone on my right hand among the serried maples. I learned over, first on one side, then on the other, to inspect my tyres, then I threw the lever.

As I flew forward, I looked ahead. There was the tall stone—on the left of the road! I was really scared and almost dazed. I meant to stop dead, take a good look at the stone, and make up my mind beyond peradventure whether it was on the right or the left— if not, indeed, in the middle of the road.

In my bewilderment I put on the highest speed. The machine leaped forward; everything I touched went wrong; I steered wildly, slewed to the left, and crashed into a big maple.

When I came to my senses, I was flat on my back in the dry ditch. The last rays of the sun sent shafts of golden-green light through the maple boughs overhead. My first thought was an odd mixture of appreciation of the beauties of nature and disapproval of my own conduct in touring without a companion—a fad I had regretted more than once. Then my mind cleared and I sat up. I felt myself from the head down. I was not bleeding; no bones were broken; and, while much shaken, I had suffered no serious bruises.

Then I saw the boy. He was standing at the edge of the cinder-path, near the ditch He was stocky and solidly built; barefoot, with his trousers rolled up to his knees; wore a sort of butternut shirt, open at the throat; and was coatless and hatless. He was tow-headed, with a shock of tousled hair; was much freckled, and had a hideous harelip. He shifted from one foot to the other, twiddled his toes, and said nothing whatever, though he stared at me intently.

I scrambled to my feet and proceeded to survey the wreck. It seemed distressingly complete. It had not blown up, nor even caught fire; but otherwise the ruin appeared hopelessly thorough. Everything I examined seemed worse smashed than the rest. My two hampers, alone, by one of those cynical jokes of chance, had escaped—both had pitched clear of the wreckage and were unhurt, not even a bottle broken.

During my investigations the boy's faded eyes followed me continuously, but he uttered no word. When I had convinced myself of my helplessness I straightened up and addressed him:

"How far is it to a blacksmith's shop?"

"Eight mile," he answered. He had a distressing case of cleft palate and was scarcely intelligible.

"Can you drive me there?" I inquired.

"Nary team on the place," he replied; "nary horse, nary cow."

"How far to the next house?" I continued.

"Six mile," he responded.

I glanced at the sky. The sun had set already. I looked at my watch: it was going—seven thirty-six.

"May I sleep in your house tonight?" I asked.

"You can come in if you want to," he said, "and sleep if you can. House all messy; Ma's been dead

37

three year, and Dad's away. Nothin' to eat but buckwheat flour and rusty bacon."

"I've plenty to eat," I answered, picking up a hamper. "Just take that hamper, will you?"

"You can come in if you've a mind to," he said, "but you got to carry your own stuff." He did not speak gruffly or rudely, but appeared mildly stating an inoffensive fact.

"All right," I said, picking up the other hamper; "lead the way."

The yard in front of the house was dark under a dozen or more immense ailanthus trees. Below them many smaller trees had grown up, and beneath these a dank underwood of tall, rank suckers out of the deep, shaggy, matted grass. What had once been, apparently, a carriage-drive, left a narrow, curved track, disused and grass-grown, leading to the house. Even here were some shoots of the ailanthus, and the air was unpleasant with the vile smell of the roots and suckers and the insistent odour of their flowers.

The house was of grey stone, with green shutters faded almost as grey as the stone. Along its front was a veranda, not much raised from the ground, and with no balustrade or railing. On it were several hickory splint rockers. There were eight shuttered windows toward the porch, and midway of them a wide door, with small violet panes on either side of it and a fanlight above.

"Open the door," I said to the boy.

"Open it yourself," he replied, not unpleasantly nor disagreeably, but in such a tone that one could not but take the suggestion as a matter of course.

I put down the two hampers and tried the door. It was latched but not locked, and opened with a rusty grind of its hinges, on which it sagged crazily, scraping the floor as it turned. The passage smelt mouldy and damp. There were several doors on either side; the boy pointed to the first on the right.

"You can have that room," he said.

I opened the door. What with the dusk, the interlacing trees outside, the piazza roof, and the closed shutters, I could make out little.

"Better get a lamp," I said to the boy.

"Nary lamp," he declared cheerfully. "Nary candle. Mostly I get abed before dark."

I returned to the remains of my conveyance. All four of my lamps were merely scrap metal and splintered glass. My lantern was mashed flat. I always, however, carried candles in my valise. This I found split and crushed, but still holding together. I carried it to the porch, opened it, and took out three candles.

Entering the room, where I found the boy standing just where I had left him, I lit the candle. The walls were whitewashed, the floor bare. There was a mildewed, chilly smell, but the bed looked freshly made up and clean, although it felt clammy.

With a few drops of its own grease I struck the candle on the corner of a mean, rickety little bureau. There was nothing else in the room save two rush-bottomed chairs and a small table. I went out on the porch, brought in my valise, and put it on the bed. I raised the sash of each window and pushed open the shutters. Then I asked the boy, who had not moved or spoken, to show me the way to the kitchen. He led me straight through the hall to the back of the house. The kitchen was large, and had no furniture save some pine chairs, a pine bench, and a pine table.

I struck two candles on opposite corners of the table. There was no stove or range in the kitchen, only a big hearth, the ashes in which smelt and looked a month old. The wood in the woodshed was dry enough, but even it had a cellary, stale smell. The axe and hatchet were both rusty and dull, but usable, and I quickly made a big fire. To my amazement, for the mid-June evening was hot and still, the boy, a wry smile on his ugly face, almost leaned over the flame, hands and arms spread out, and fairly roasted himself.

"Are you cold?" I inquired.

"I'm allus cold," he replied, hugging the fire closer than ever, till I thought he must scorch.

I left him toasting himself while I went in search of water. I discovered the pump, which was in working order and not dry on the valves; but I had a furious struggle to fill the two leaky pails I had found. When I had put water to boil I fetched my hampers from the porch.

I brushed the table and set out my meal—cold fowl, cold ham, white and brown bread, olives, jam, and cake. When the can of soup was hot and the coffee made I drew up two chairs to the table and invited the boy to join me.

"I ain't hungry," he said; "I've had supper."

He was a new sort of boy to me; all the boys I knew were hearty eaters and always ready. I had felt hungry myself, but somehow when I came to eat I had little appetite and hardly relished the food. I soon made an end of my meal, covered the fire, blew out the candles, and returned to the porch, where I dropped into one of the hickory rockers to smoke. The boy followed me silently and seated himself on the porch floor, leaning against a pillar, his feet on the grass outside.

"What do you do," I asked, "when your father is away?"

"Just loaf 'round," he said. "Just fool 'round."

"How far off are your nearest neighbours?" I asked.

"Don't no neighbours never come here," he stated. "Say they're afeared of the ghosts."

I was not at all startled; the place had all those aspects which lead to a house being called haunted. I was struck by his odd matter-of-fact way of speaking— it was as if he had said they were afraid of a cross dog.

"Do you ever see any ghosts around here?" I continued.

"Never see 'em," he answered, as if I had mentioned tramps or partridges. "Never hear 'em. Sort o' feel 'em 'round sometimes."

"Are you afraid of them?" I asked.

"Nope," he declared. "I ain't skeered o' ghosts; I'm skeered o' nightmares. Ever have nightmares?"

"Very seldom," I replied.

"I do," he returned. "Allus have the same nightmare—big sow, big as a steer, trying to eat me up. Wake up so skeered I could run to never. Nowheres to run to. Go to sleep, and have it again. Wake up worse skeered than ever. Dad says it's buckwheat cakes in summer."

"You must have teased a sow some time." I said.

"Yep," he answered. "Teased a big sow wunst, holding up one of her pigs by the hind leg. Teased her too long. Fell in the pen and got bit up some. Wisht I hadn't a' teased her. Have that nightmare three times a week sometimes. Worse'n being burnt out. Worse'n ghosts. Say, I sorter feel ghosts around now."

He was not trying to frighten me. He was as simply stating an opinion as if he had spoken of bats or mosquitoes. I made no reply, and found myself listening involuntarily. My pipe went out. I did not really want another, but felt disinclined for bed as yet, and was comfortable where I was, while the smell of the ailanthus blossoms was very disagreeable. I filled my pipe again, lit it, and then, as I puffed, somehow dozed off for a moment.

I awoke with a sensation of some light fabric trailed across my face. The boy's position was unchanged.

"Did you do that?" I asked sharply.

"Ain't done nary thing," he rejoined. "What was it?"

"It was like a piece of mosquito-netting brushed over my face."

"That ain't netting," he asserted; "that's a veil. That's one of the ghosts. Some blow on you; some touch you with their long, cold fingers. That one with the veil she drags acrosst your face—well, mostly I think it's Ma."

He spoke with the unassailable conviction of the child in *We Are Seven*. I found no words to reply, and rose to go to bed.

"Goodnight," I said.

42

"Goodnight," he echoed. "I'll sit out here a spell yet."

I lit a match, found the candle I had stuck on the corner of the shabby little bureau, and undressed. The bed had a comfortable husk mattress. and I was soon asleep.

I had the sensation of having slept some time when I had a nightmare—the very nightmare the boy had described. A huge sow, big as a dray horse, was reared up with her forelegs over the foot-board of the bed, trying to scramble over to me. She grunted and puffed, and I felt I was the food she craved. I knew in the dream that it was only a dream, and strove to wake up.

Then the gigantic dream-beast floundered over the footboard, fell across my shins, and I awoke.

I was in darkness as absolute as if I were sealed in a jet vault, yet the shudder of the nightmare instantly subsided, my nerves quieted; I realised where I was, and felt not the least panic. I turned over and was asleep again almost at once. Then I had a real nightmare, not recognisable as a dream, but appallingly real—an unutterable agony of reasonless horror.

There was a Thing in the room; not a sow, nor any other nameable creature, but a Thing. It was as big as an elephant, filled the room to the ceiling, was shaped like a wild boar, seated on its haunches, with its forelegs braced stiffly in front of it. It had a hot, slobbering, red mouth, full of big tusks, and its jaws worked hungrily. It shuffled and hunched itself forward, inch by inch, till its vast forelegs straddled the bed.

The bed crushed up like wet blotting-paper, and I

felt the weight of the Thing on my feet, on my legs, on my body, on my chest. It was hungry, and I was what it was hungry for, and it meant to begin on my face. Its dripping mouth was nearer and nearer.

Then the dream-helplessness that made me unable to call or move suddenly gave way, and I yelled and awoke. This time my terror was positive and not to be shaken off.

It was near dawn: I could descry dimly the cracked, dirty window-panes. I got up, lit the stump of my candle and two fresh ones, dressed hastily, strapped my ruined valise, and put it on the porch against the wall near the door. Then I called the boy. I realised quite suddenly that I had not told him my name or asked his.

I shouted "Hallo!" a few times, but won no answer. I had had enough of that house. I was still permeated with the panic of the nightmare. I desisted from shouting, made no search, but with two candles went out to the kitchen. I took a swallow of cold coffee and munched a biscuit as I hustled my belongings into my hampers. Then, leaving a silver dollar on the table, I carried the hampers out on the porch and dumped them by my valise.

It was now light enough to see to walk, and I went out to the road. Already the night-dew had rusted much of the wreck, making it look more hopeless than before. It was, however, entirely undisturbed. There was not so much as a wheel-track or a hoof-print on the road. The tall, white stone, uncertainty about which had caused my disaster, stood like a sentinel opposite where I had upset.

I set out to find that blacksmith shop. Before I had gone far the sun rose clear from the horizon, and was almost at once scorching. As I footed it along I grew very much heated, and it seemed more like ten miles than six before I reached the first house. It was a new frame house, neatly painted and close to the road, with a whitewashed fence along its garden front.

I was about to open the gate when a big black dog with a curly tail bounded out of the bushes. He did not bark but stood inside the gate wagging his tail and regarding me with a friendly eye; yet I hesitated with my hand on the latch and considered. The dog might not be as friendly as he looked, and the sight of him made me realise that except for the boy I had seen no creature about the house where I had spent the night; no dog or cat; not even a toad or bird. While I was ruminating upon this a man came from behind the house.

"Will your dog bite?" I asked.

"Naw," he answered; "he don't bite. Come in."

I told him I had had an accident to my automobile, and asked if he could drive me to the blacksmith's shop and back to my wreckage.

"Cert," he said. "Happy to help you. I'll hitch up foreshortly. Where'd you smash?"

"In front of the grey house about six miles back," I answered.

"That big stone-built house?" he queried.

"The same," I assented.

"Did you go a-past here?" he inquired astonished. "I didn't hear ye."

"No," I said; "I came from the other direction."

"Why," he meditated, "you must'a' smashed about sunup. Did you come over them mountains in the dark?"

"No," I replied; "I came over them yesterday evening. I smashed up about sunset."

"Sundown!" he exclaimed. "Where in thunder've ye been all night?"

"I slept in the house where I broke down."

"In that big stone-built house in the trees?" he demanded.

"Yes," I agreed.

"Why," he quavered excitedly, "that there house is haunted! They say if you have to drive past it after dark, you can't tell which side of the road the big white stone is on."

"I couldn't tell even before sunset," I said.

"There!" he exclaimed. "Look at that, now! And you slep' in that house! Did you sleep, honest?"

"I slept pretty well," I said. "Except for a nightmare, I slept all night."

"Well," he commented, "I wouldn't go in that there house for a farm, nor sleep in it for my salvation. And you slep'! How in thunder did you get in?"

"The boy took me in," I said.

"What sort of a boy?" he queried, his eyes fixed on me with a queer, countrified look of absorbed interest.

"A thick-set, freckle-faced boy with a hare-lip," I said.

"Talk like his mouth was full of mush?" he demanded.

"Yes," I said; "bad case of cleft palate."

"Well!" he exclaimed. "I never did believe in

46

ghosts, and I never did half believe that house was haunted, but I know it now. And you slep'!"

"I didn't see any ghosts," I retorted irritably.

"You seen a ghost for sure," he rejoined solemnly. "That there harelip boy's been dead six months."

From *Lukandoo And Other Stories* by Edward Lucas White (Dodd, Mead & Co., New York).

THE STORY OF THE INEXPERIENCED GHOST

By H. G. WELLS

THE SCENE amidst which Clayton told his last story comes back very vividly to my mind. There he sat, for the greater part of the time, in the corner of the authentic settle by the spacious open fire, and Sanderson sat beside him smoking the Broseley clay that bore his name. There was Evans, and that marvel among actors, Wish, who is also a modest man. We had all come down to the Mermaid Club that Saturday morning, except Clayton, who had slept there overnight—which indeed gave him the opening of his story. We had golfed until golfing was invisible; we had dined, and we were in that mood of tranquil kindliness when men will suffer a story. When Clayton began to tell one, we naturally supposed he was lying. It may be that indeed he was lying—of that the reader

47

will speedily be able to judge as well as I. He began, it is true, with an air of matter-of-fact anecdote, but that we thought was only the incurable artifice of the man.

"I say!" he remarked, after a long consideration of the upward rain of sparks from the log that Sanderson had thumped, "you know I was alone here last night?"

"Except for the domestics," said Wish.

"Who sleep in the other wing," said Clayton. "Yes. Well——" He pulled at his cigar for some little time as though he still hesitated about his confidence. Then he said, quite quietly, "I caught a ghost!"

"Caught a ghost, did you?" said Sanderson. "Where is it?"

And Evans, who admires Clayton immensely and has been four weeks in America, shouted, "*Caught* a ghost, did you, Clayton? I'm glad of it! Tell us all about it right now."

Clayton said he would in a minute, and asked him to shut the door.

He looked apologetically at me. "There's no eavesdropping, of course, but we don't want to upset our very excellent service with any rumours of ghosts in the place. There's too much shadow and oak panelling to trifle with that. And this, you know, wasn't a regular ghost. I don't think it will come again —ever."

"You mean to say you didn't keep it?" said Sanderson.

"I hadn't the heart to," said Clayton.

And Sanderson said he was surprised.

We laughed, and Clayton looked aggrieved. "I know," he said, with a flicker of a smile, "but the fact is it really *was* a ghost, and I'm as sure of it as I am that I am talking to you now. I'm not joking. I mean what I say."

Sanderson drew deeply at his pipe, with one reddish eye on Clayton, and then emitted a thin jet of smoke more eloquent than many words.

Clayton ignored the comment. "It is the strangest thing that has ever happened in my life. You know I never believed in ghosts or anything of the sort, before, ever; and then, you know, I bag one in a corner; and the whole business is in my hands."

He meditated still more profoundly and produced, and began to pierce, a second cigar with a curious little stabber he affected.

"You talked to it?" asked Wish.

"For the space, probably, of an hour."

'Chatty?" I said, joining the party of sceptics.

"The poor devil was in trouble," said Clayton, bowed over his cigar-end and with the very faintest note of reproof.

"Sobbing?" someone asked.

Clayton heaved a realistic sigh at the memory. "Good Lord!" he said; "yes." And then, "Poor fellow! Yes."

"Where did you strike it?" asked Evans, in his best American accent.

"I never realised," said Clayton, ignoring him, "the poor sort of thing a ghost might be," and he hung us up again for a time, while he sought for matches in his pocket and lit and warmed to his cigar.

"I took an advantage," he reflected at last.

We were none of us in a hurry. "A character," he

said, "remains just the same character for all that it's been disembodied. That's a thing we too often forget. People with a certain strength or fixity of purpose may have ghosts of a certain strength and fixity of purpose —most haunting ghosts, you know, must be as one-idea'd as monomaniacs and as obstinate as mules to come back again and again. This poor creature wasn't." He suddenly looked up rather queerly, and his eye went round the room. "I say it," he said, "in all kindliness, but that is the plain truth of the case. Even at the first glance he struck me as weak."

He punctuated with the help of his cigar.

"I came upon him, you know, in the long passage. His back was towards me and I saw him first. Right off I knew him for a ghost. He was transparent and whitish; clean through his chest I could see the glimmer of the little window at the end. And not only his physique but his attitude struck me as being weak. He looked, you know, as though he didn't know in the slightest whatever he meant to do. One hand was on the panelling and the other fluttered to his mouth. Like—*so!*"

"What sort of physique?" said Sanderson.

"Lean. You know that sort of young man's neck that has two great flutings down the back, here and here—so! And a little, meanish head with scrubby hair and rather bad ears. Shoulders bad, narrower than the hips; turn-down collar, ready-made short jacket,, trousers baggy and a little frayed at the heels. That's how he took me. I came very quietly up the staircase. I did not carry a light, you know—the candles are on the landing table and there is that lamp

"Are you a member?" I said

—and I was in my list slippers, and I saw him as I came up. I stopped dead at that—taking him in. I wasn't a bit afraid. I think that in most of these affairs one is never nearly so afraid or excited as one imagines one would be. I was surprised and interested. I thought, 'Good Lord! Here's a ghost as last! And I haven't believed for a moment in ghosts during the last five-and-twenty years'."

"Um," said Wish.

"I suppose I wasn't on the landing a moment before he found out I was there. He turned on me sharply, and I saw the face of an immature young man, a weak nose, a scrubby little moustache, a feeble chin. So for an instant we stood—he looking over his shoulder at me—and regarded one another. Then he seemed to remember his high calling. He turned round, drew himself up, projected his face, raised his arms, spread his hands in approved ghost fashion—came towards me. As he did so his little jaw dropped, and he emitted a faint, drawn-out 'Boo.' It wasn't—not a bit dreadful. I'd dined. I'd had a bottle of champagne, and being all alone, perhaps two or three—perhaps even four or five —whiskies, so I was as solid as rocks and no more frightened than if I'd been assailed by a frog. 'Boo!' I said. 'Nonsense. You don't belong to *this* place. What are you doing here?'

"I could see him wince. 'Boo-oo,' he said.

"'Boo—be hanged! Are you a member?' I said; and just to show I didn't care a pin for him I stepped through a corner of him and made to light my candle. 'Are you a member?' I repeated, looking at him sideways.

"He moved a little so as to stand clear of me, and his bearing became crestfallen. 'No,' he said, in answer to the persistent interrogation of my eye; 'I'm not a member—I'm a ghost.'

"'Well, that doesn't give you the run of the Mermaid Club. Is there anyone you want to see, or anything of that sort?' And doing it as steadily as possible for fear that he should mistake the carelessness of whisky for the distraction of fear, I got my candle alight. I turned on him, holding it. 'What are you doing here?' I said.

"He had dropped his hands and stopped his booing, and there he stood, abashed and awkward, the ghost of a weak, silly, aimless young man. 'I'm haunting,' he said.

"'You haven't any business to,' I said, in a quiet voice.

"'I'm a ghost,' he said, as if in defence.

"'That may be, but you haven't any business to haunt here. This is a respectable private club; people often stop here with nursemaids and children, and, going about in the careless way you do, some poor little mite could easily come upon you and be scared out of her wits. I suppose you didn't think of that?'

"'No, sir,' he said, 'I didn't.'

"'You should have done. You haven't any claim on the place, have you? Weren't murdered here, or anything of that sort?'

"'None, sir; but I thought as it was old and oak-panelled——'

"'That's *no* excuse.' I regarded him firmly. 'Your coming here is a mistake,' I said, in a tone of friendly
53

superiority. I feigned to see if I had my matches, and then looked up at him frankly. 'If I were you, I wouldn't wait for cock-crow—I'd vanish right away.'

"He looked embarrassed. 'The fact *is*, sir——' he began.

" 'I'd vanish,' I said, driving it home.

" 'The fact is, sir, that—somehow—I can't.'

" 'You *can't?*'

" 'No, sir. There's something I've forgotten. I've been hanging about here since midnight last night, hiding in the cupboards of the empty bedrooms and things like that. I'm flurried. I've never come haunting before, and it seems to put me out.'

" 'Put you out?'

" 'Yes, sir. I've tried to do it several times, and it doesn't come off. There's some little thing has slipped me, and I can't get back.'

"That, you know, rather bowled me over. He looked at me in such an abject way that for the life of me I couldn't keep up quite the high, hectoring vein I had adopted. 'That's queer,' I said, and, as I spoke. I fancied I heard someone moving about down below. "Come into my room and tell me more about it,' I said. I didn't, of course, understand this, and I tried to take him by the arm. But, of course, you might as well have tried to take hold of a puff of smoke! I had forgotten my number, I think; anyhow, I remember going into several bedrooms—it was lucky I was the only soul in that wing—until I saw my traps. 'Here we are,' I said, and sat down in the armchair; 'sit down and tell me all about it. It seems to me you have got yourself into a jolly awkward position, old chap.'

"Well, he said he wouldn't sit down; he'd prefer to flit up and down the room if it was all the same to me. And so he did, and in a little while we were deep in a long and serious talk. And presently, you know, something of those whiskies and sodas evaporated out of me, and I began to realise just a little what a thundering rum and weird business it was that I was in. There he was, semi-transparent—the proper conventional phantom, and noiseless except for his ghost of a voice—flitting to and fro in that nice, clean, chintz-hung old bedroom. You could see the gleam of the copper candlesticks through him, and the lights on the brass fender, and the corners of the framed engravings on the wall, and there he was telling me all about this wretched little life of his that had recently ended on Earth. He hadn't a particularly honest face, you know, but being transparent, of course, he couldn't avoid telling the truth."

"Eh?" said Wish, suddenly sitting up in his chair.

"What?" said Clayton.

"Being transparent—couldn't avoid telling the truth —I don't see it," said Wish.

"*I* don't see it," said Clayton, with inimitable assurance. "But it *is* so, I can assure you, nevertheless. I don't believe he got once a nail's breadth off the Bible truth. He told me how he had been killed—he went down into a London basement with a candle to look for a leakage of gas—and described himself as a senior English master in a London private school when that release occurred."

"Poor wretch!" said I.

"That's what I thought, and the more he talked the

55

more I thought it. There he was, purposeless in life and purposeless out of it. He talked of his father and mother and his schoolmaster, and all who had ever been anything to him in the world, meanly. He had been too sensitive, too nervous; none of them had ever valued him properly or understood him, he said. He had never had a real friend in the world, I think; he had never had a success. He had shirked games and failed examinations. 'It's like that with some people,' he said; 'whenever I got into the examination-room or anywhere, everything seemed to go.' Engaged to be married, of course—to another over-sensitive person, I suppose—when the indiscretion with the gas escape ended his affairs. 'And where are you now?' I asked. 'Not in——?'

"He wasn't clear on that point at all. The impression he gave me was a sort of vague, intermediate state, a special reserve for souls too non-existent for anything so positive as either sin or virtue. *I* don't know. He was much too egotistical and unobservant to give me any clear idea of the kind of place, kind of country, there is on the Other Side of Things. Wherever he was he seems to have fallen in with a set of kindred spirits: ghosts of weak Cockney young men, who were on a footing of Christian names, and among these there was certainly a lot of talk about 'going haunting' and things like that. Yes—going haunting! They seemed to think haunting a tremendous adventure, and most of them funked it all the time. And so primed, you know, he had come."

"But really!" said Wish to the fire.

"These are the impressions he gave me, anyhow,"

said Clayton modestly. "I may, of course, have been in a rather uncritical state, but that was the sort of background he gave to himself. He kept flitting up and down, with his thin voice going—talking, talking about his wretched self, and never a word of clear, firm statement from first to last. He was thinner and sillier and more pointless than if he had been real and alive. Only then, you know, he would not have been in my bedroom here—if he *had* been alive. I should have kicked him out."

"Of course," said Evans, "there *are* poor mortals like that."

"And there's just as much chance of their having ghosts as the rest of us," I admitted.

"What gave a sort of point to him, you know, was the fact that he did seem within limits to have found himself out. The mess he had made of haunting had depressed him terribly. He had been told it would be a 'lark'; he had come expecting it to be a 'lark,' and here it was, nothing but another failure added to his record! He proclaimed himself an utter out-and-out failure. He said, and I can quite believe it, that he had never tried to do anything all his life that he hadn't made a perfect mess of—and through all the wastes of eternity he never would. If he had had sympathy, perhaps—— He paused at that, and stood regarding me. He remarked that, strange as it might seem to me, nobody, not any one, ever, had given him the amount of sympathy I was doing now. I could see what he wanted straight away, and I determined to head him off at once. I may be a brute, you know, but being the Only Real Friend, the recipient of the confidences of one of these egotistical weaklings, ghost or body, is beyond my physical endurance. I got up briskly. 'Don't you brood on these things too much,' I said. 'The thing you've got to do is to get out of this—get out of this sharp. You pull yourself together and *try*.' 'I can't,' he said. 'You try,' I said, and try he did."

"Try!" said Sanderson. *"How?"*

"Passes," said Clayton.

'Passes?"

"Complicated series of gestures and passes with the hands. That's how he had come in and that's how he had to get out again. Lord! What a business I had!"

"But how could *any* series of passes——" I began.

"My dear man," said Clayton, turning on me and putting a great emphasis on certain words, "you want *everything* clear. *I* don't know *how*. All I know is that you *do*—that *he* did, anyhow, at least. After a fearful time, you know, he got his passes right and suddenly disappeared."

"Did you," said Sanderson, slowly, "observe the passes?"

"Yes," said Clayton, and seemed to think. "It was tremendously queer," he said. "There we were, I and this thin vague ghost, in that silent room, in this silent, empty inn, in this silent little Friday-night town. Not a sound except our voices and a faint panting he made when he swung. There was the bedroom candle, and one candle on the dressing-table alight, that was all—sometimes one or other would flare up into a tall, lean, astonished flame for a space. And queer things happened. 'I can't,' he said; 'I shall never——!' And suddenly he sat down on a little chair at the foot of the

58

bed and began to sob and sob. Lord! What a harrowing, whimpering thing he seemed!

" 'You pull yourself together,' I said, and tried to pat him on the back, and . . . my confounded hand went through him! By that time, you know, I wasn't nearly so—massive as I had been on the landing. I got the queerness of it full. I remember snatching back my hand out of him, as it were, with a little thrill, and walking over to the dressing-table. 'You pull yourself together,' I said to him, 'and try.' And in order to encourage and help him, I began to try as well."

"What!" said Sanderson, "the passes?"

"Yes, the passes."

"But——" I said, moved by an idea that eluded me for a pace.

"This is interesting," said Sanderson, with his finger in his pipe-bowl. "You mean to say this ghost of yours gave away——"

"Did his level best to give away the whole confounded barrier? *Yes.*"

"He didn't," said Wish; "he couldn't. Or you'd have gone there too."

"That's precisely it," I said, finding my elusive idea put into words for me.

"That *is* precisely it," said Clayton, with thoughtful eyes upon the fire.

For just a little while there was silence.

"And at last he did it?" said Sanderson.

"At last he did it. I had to keep him up to it hard, but he did it at last—rather suddenly. He despaired, we had a scene, and then he got up abruptly and asked me to go through the whole performance, slowly, so

59

that he might see. 'I believe,' he said, 'if I could *see* I should spot what was wrong at once.' And he did. '*I* know,' he said. 'What do you know?' said I. '*I* know,' he repeated. Then he said peevishly, 'I *can't* do it if you look at me—I really *can't*; it's been that, partly, all along. I'm such a nervous fellow that you put me out.' Well, we had a bit of an argument. Naturally, I wanted to see; but he was as obstinate as a mule, and suddenly I had come over as tired as a dog—he tired me out. 'All right,' I said, '*I* won't look at you,' and turned towards the mirror, on the wardrobe, by the bed.

"He started off very fast. I tried to follow him by looking in the looking-glass, to see just what it was had gone wrong. Round went his arms and hands, so, and so, and so, and then with a rush came to the last gesture of all—you stand erect and open out your arms—and so, don't you know, he stood. And then he didn't! He didn't! He wasn't! I wheeled round from the looking-glass to him. There was nothing! I was alone with the flaring candles and a staggering mind. What had happened? Had anything happened? Had I been dreaming? . . . And then, with an absurd note of finality about it, the clock upon the landing discovered the moment was ripe for striking *one*. So!—Ping! And I was as grave and sober as a judge, with all my champagne and whisky gone into the vast serene. Feeling queer, you know—confoundedly *queer!* Queer! Good Lord!"

He regarded his cigar-ash for a moment. "That's all that happened," he said.

"And then you went to bed?" asked Evans.

"What else was there to do?"

I looked Wish in the eye. We wanted to scoff, and there was something, something perhaps in Clayton's voice and manner, that hampered our desire.

"And about these passes?" said Sanderson.

"I believe I could do them now."

"Oh!" said Sanderson, and produced a pen-knife and set himself to grub the dottle out of the bowl of his clay.

"Why don't you do them now?" said Sanderson, shutting his pen-knife with a click.

"That's what I'm going to do," said Clayton.

"They won't work," said Evans.

"If they do——" I suggested.

"You know, I'd rather you didn't," said Wish, stretching out his legs.

"Why?" asked Evans.

"I'd rather he didn't." said Wish.

"But he hasn't got 'em right," said Sanderson, plugging too much tobacco into his pipe.

"All the same, I'd rather he didn't," said Wish.

We argued with Wish. He said that for Clayton to go through those gestures was like mocking a serious matter. "But you don't believe——?" I said. Wish glanced at Clayton, who was staring into the fire, weighing something in his mind. "I do—more than half, anyhow, I do," said Wish.

"Clayton," said I, "you're too good a liar for us. Most of it was all right. But that disappearance . . . happened to be convincing. Tell us, it's a tale of cock and bull."

He stood up without heeding me, took the middle of the hearthrug, and faced me. For a moment he regarded his feet thoughtfully, and then for all the rest of the time his eyes were on the opposite wall, with an intent expression. He raised his two hands slowly to the level of his eyes and so began . . .

Now, Sanderson is a Freemason, a member of the lodge of the Four Kings, which devotes itself so ably to the study and elucidation of all the mysteries of Masonry past and present, and among the students of this lodge Sanderson is by no means the least. He followed Clayton's motions with a singular interest in his reddish eye. "That's not bad," he said, when it was done. "You really do, you know, put things together, Clayton, in a most amazing fashion. But there's one little detail out."

"I know," said Clayton. "I believe I could tell you which."

"Well?"

"This," said Clayton, and did a queer little twist and writhing and thrust of the hands.

"Yes."

"That, you know, was what *he* couldn't get right," said Clayton. "But how do *you*——?"

"Most of this business, and particularly how you invented it, I don't understand at all," said Sanderson, "but just that phase—I do." He reflected. "These happen to be a series of gestures—concerned with a certain branch of esoteric Masonry—— Probably you know. Or else—— *How?*" He reflected still further. "I do not see I can do any harm in telling you just the proper twist. After all, if you know, you know; if you don't, you don't."

"I know nothing," said Clayton, "except what the poor devil let out last night."

"Well, anyhow," said Sanderson, and placed his churchwarden very carefully upon the shelf over the fireplace. Then very rapidly he gesticulated with his hands.

"So?" said Clayton, repeating.

"So," said Sanderson, and took his pipe in hand again.

"Ah, *now*," said Clayton, "I can do the whole thing — right."

He stood up before the waning fire and smiled at us all. But I think there was just a little hesitation in his smile. "If I begin——" he said.

"I wouldn't begin," said Wish.

"It's all right!" said Evans. "Matter is indestructible. You don't think any jiggery-pokery of this sort is going to snatch Clayton into the world of shades. Not it! You may try, Clayton, so far as I'm concerned, until your arms drop off at the wrists."

"I don't believe that," said Wish, and stood up and put his arm on Clayton's shoulder. "You've made me half believe in that story somehow, and I don't want to see the thing done."

"Goodness!" said I, "here's Wish frightened!"

"I am," said Wish, with real or admirably feigned intensity. "I believe that if he goes through these motions right, he'll *go*."

"He'll not do anything of the sort," I cried. "There's only one way out of this world for men, and Clayton is thirty years from that. Besides . . . And such a ghost! Do you think——?"

Wish interrupted me by moving. He walked out from among our chairs and stopped beside the table and stood there. "Clayton," he said, "you're a fool."

Clayton, with a humorous light in his eyes, smiled back at him. "Wish," he said, "is right and all you others are wrong. I shall go. I shall get to the end of these passes, and as the last swish whistles through the air, Presto!—this hearthrug will be vacant, the room will be blank amazement, and a respectably dressed gentleman of fifteen stone will plump into the world of shades. I'm certain. So will you be. I decline to argue further. Let the thing be tried."

"No," said Wish, and made a step and ceased, and Clayton raised his hands once more to repeat the spirit's passing.

By that time, you know, we were all in a state of tension—largely because of the behaviour of Wish. We sat all of us with our eyes on Clayton—I, at least, with a sort of tight, stiff feeling about me as though from the back of my skull to the middle of my thighs my body had been changed to steel. And there, with a gravity that was imperturbably serene, Clayton bowed and swayed and waved his hands and arms before us. As he drew towards the end one piled up, one tingled in one's teeth. The last gesture, I have said, was to swing the arms out wide open, with the face held up. And when at last he swung out to this closing gesture, I ceased even to breathe. It was ridiculous, of course, but you know that ghost-story feeling. It was after dinner, in a queer, old shadowy house. Would he, after all——?

There he stood for one stupendous moment, with his

arms open and his upturned face, assured and bright, in the glare of the hanging lamp. We hung through that moment as if it were an age, and then came from all of us something that was half a sigh of infinite relief and half a reassuring *"No!"* For visibly—he wasn't going. It was all nonsense. He had told an idle story, and carried it almost to conviction, that was all! . . . And then in that moment the face of Clayton changed.

It changed. It changed as a lit house changes when its lights are suddenly extinguished. His eyes were suddenly eyes that were fixed, his smile was frozen on his lips, and he stood there still. He stood there, very gently swaying.

That moment, too, was an age. And then, you know, chairs were scraping, things were falling, and we were all moving. His knees seemed to give, and he fell forward, and Evans rose and caught him in his arms . . .

It stunned us all. For a minute, I suppose, no one said a coherent thing. We believed it, yet could not believe it . . . I came out of a muddled stupefaction to find myself kneeling beside him, and his vest and shirt were torn open, and Sanderson's hand lay on his heart . . .

Well—the simple fact before us could very well wait our convenience; there was no hurry for us to comprehend. It lay there for an hour; it lies athwart my memory, black and amazing still, to this day. Clayton had, indeed, passed into the world that lies so near to and so far from our own, and he had gone thither by the only road that mortal man may take.

C

But whether he did indeed pass there by the poor ghost's incantation, or whether he was stricken suddenly by apoplexy in the midst of an idle tale—as the coroner's jury would have us believe—is no matter for my judging; it is just one of those inexplicable riddles that must remain unsolved until the final solution of all things shall come. All I certainly know is that, in the very moment, in the very instant, of concluding those passes, he changed, and staggered, and fell down before us—dead!

THE GIANT BONES

By SORCHE NIC LEODHAS

ONCE IN the old, old days long since gone, there dwelt a race of giants in the land of Caledonia, which was the name folk had for Scotland then. Whatever happened to them nobody knows, although many an old tale is told about it. Some say they went along with Angus Og when he went away with the weight of sorrow on his shoulders because of the evil doings of man. Some will tell you the giant folk battled among themselves until they had all killed each other off. And there are still others who will tell you that a great beast rose up from the sea and ate all of them up. They're all grand stories, and you can believe what you like and no one will be faulting you for it, because no one will know any more about it than yourself. One thing is certain:

gone they are, the whole lot of them, and naught left behind them but some huge bones that show what big-sized creatures they were when they walked about in their flesh.

They say these bones are to be found in a great cave near the causeway at the far northern tip of Scotland. The man who found them first ran off screaming. He never was the same again, for he swore that as he bent over to look at what might have been a knucklebone—and it half as big as himself—he gave it a sharp rap with the toe of his boot. It was all by accident, for he didn't mean to at all. And, according to the way he tells the story, something moved across the cave, and a great voice roared at him.

"Och now!" it said. "Will ye not take heed to yourself, wee man o' the people, that ye'll not be disturbing honest folk in their sleep!"

The man looked all round him and all round the cave. He could see plain enough by the light from the sea waves, where the sun danced upon them near the opening that there was nobody in the place but himself alone. But he could *feel* that there was something there, and it was coming right at him! 'Twas then he screamed and ran away.

As it was the most important event of his life, he told the tale of it over and over, and is still telling it to whoever will stop to listen, for all anyone knows. But one thing he'd never tell and that was where the cave with the giant bones was to be found. He had a dread on him that the telling of it would set whatever it was in the cave after him.

Folk that dwelt thereabouts got used to his story and

finally they got tired of it. But he was always able to find someone to listen to it, because the place he lived in was a grand one for the shooting and fishing folk from below the border who came up for their holidays. That way, it wasn't hard to find a new pair of ears that hadn't heard him tell about the cave with the giant bones.

Well, at last he told the tale to a man who was new to the place and had never even been in Scotland before. This stranger was one of those fellows who work at gathering fossils and old bones and the like, and looking into ruined places to find out what sort of folks had belonged to them maybe hundreds of years ago. When he found out enough, he'd make a book out of his knowledge and people would buy the book and pay good money for it. Which was why he wrote it, of course.

When the stranger heard about the giant bones, he was bound to make a book about them. The trouble was that nobody but the man who had found them knew where they were, and he wasn't telling.

The stranger flew into a rage and said nobody need tell him, for he'd just find the cave for himself.

Well, he searched up and he searched down all along the seacoast, and he found a terrible lot of caves; but not one of the lot had any sort of bones except those of sea birds in it, nor anything else that would have paid him back for the time he'd spent looking.

Finally, there wasn't so much as a hole in a rock he hadn't looked into, and he'd take his oath that there wasn't a cave anywhere that he'd missed. There was a suspicion in his mind that the whole story was a pack o' nonsense all made up in the mind of the man who'd told it to him.

He climbed up to the top of the cliff and began to walk back towards the place where he was staying. It was easier walking up there than over the shale along the shore. Climbing in and out of caves had made him hot and weary, and he was that mad because he thought he'd been made a fool of. He was walking along, with his mind busy with what he was going to say to the man whose story had sent him after the bones, so maybe he wasn't watching where he was going. At any rate, all of a sudden the ground crumbled under him, and down he shot over the cliff's edge in the midst of a great shower of dirt and stones.

He landed on a great heap of rubble with the breath knocked clean out of him. He soon found he wasn't hurt badly, so as soon as he got his breath back he sat up to see where he was. The sea came up to the foot of the pile of stuff he was sitting on and at either side of him was a great boulder towering halfway up the cliff. But it wasn't the boulders that held his eye. Between the two of them was the opening to a cave. He'd never seen either boulders or opening before, and he couldn't see how he'd missed them, but he wasted no time trying to work out why. Up he got and into the cave he ran.

It was the right one! There were the giant bones lying all over the floor just as the man had told him.

'Twas the sight to gladden the eye of one who earned his bread poking his nose into old bones and the like. He started at once to sort them out, thinking that if he could get a whole man laid out 'twould make a grand picture for the book he was going to write. So being busy at it, he paid no heed to anything else, until a great rumbling voice roared in his ears, and the voice said, *"Leave the bones be, man!"*

Losh! The stranger leapt a foot in the air for fright. When he came down, he tripped over one of the bones he'd been sorting out and landed with a thump on a couple more. And another thundering voice shouted, "Och, ye clumsy lout! Will you not stop booting my poor old bones about!"

The stranger was so near dead with fright that he scarce had the strength to lift his head to see who was speaking. When he did, he'd have been better pleased if he'd not looked at all. All around the cave, reaching all the way from the floor to the top of it, stood a ring of ghosts. They were the biggest ghosts anyone ever saw. The cave was so big you could have drilled a regiment in it easy and with room to spare; but they made it feel crowded, they were that huge.

There was no place he could run because he was in the midst of them, and they gathered around him as they were, shoulder to shoulder and toe to toe. So he lay there looking up at them, with his blood grueing and himself shaking like a leaf in the wind.

"What shall we do wi' the wee sma' man!" roared one of the great ghosts.

"Crock him!" answered another, in a voice that nearly split the stranger's lugs.

"Let me at him!" shouted a third of them. "I'll be taking him apart, so I will, to spread his wee bones amongst our own. 'Twas my shin he was knocking a while back, so it was!"

"Och nay!" thundered the biggest of them all. "Would we be having the puny bones of him cluttering up the place? Let's be rid of him!"

"Let's be rid of him!" they all agreed, and their combined voices bouncing around the cave sounded like thunder along mountain tops.

Before the stranger could get himself to his knees to beg for mercy, he felt something pick him up, and there was a great swirling and booming. Out of the cave he flew, as if carried by a whirlwind, spinning like a top through the air, and into the sea he fell.

He'd have drowned, if it had not been for some fishermen who heard the splash he made. They turned their boats, came up to him, and fished him out of the sea more dead than alive.

When they brought him to, he tried to tell them about the terrible experience he'd had. But they only laughed at him and told him that people getting drowned always had strange fancies afterwards. He'd fallen into the sea from the cliff above. That was all.

The stranger never wrote the book, for he had no wish to be poking his nose into those bones again. But the story spread around, and curious people went to look for the cave. They never found it. All they found was the two huge boulders, and they were set close together, and half of them buried in the cliff. Some people said it was plain to be seen they'd been that way a hundred years or more. Some people said the giant ghosts had pushed them there to bar the door of the cave so they could rest in peace. However it was, you can go and look at the place yourself. They'll show you the boulders and tell you there's a cave behind them full of giant ghosts guarding their giant bones.

PRINCE GODFREY FREES MOUNTAIN DWELLERS AND LITTLE SHEPHERDS FROM A SAVAGE WEREWOLF AND FROM WITCHES

By HALINA GORSKA

A SHORT time after the disappearance of the shepherd's pet had involved Godfrey in his adventure with the elves, two other goats went astray, then a ram and four sheep, and last a large white cow, the pride of the whole herd.

The old herdsman brooded greatly over this loss and was particularly disconsolate over the cow. He was angry at the herdboys because they had a mind for nothing but pranks, he said, and could not keep their animals from harm.

When, however, shortly after that, a bull was lost, too, a bull so strong and stubborn that he would have been a match for any wolf, the old man shook his head sadly and said, "Ah, boys, 'tis some unholy power and not the wolves. As long as only goats and sheep were lost, I thought it was your carelessness that was to blame, for it is well known that they are foolish, flighty and thoughtless creatures and likely to come to grief, so that they want careful watching. But with a cow it is an altogether different matter. And what a cow, mind you. Quiet, sedate, not at all given to pranks and frolic. Still, I said to myself that even such a cow might be frightened into straying from the herd, and in the woods a mishap is easily met with. But a bull. Why, he would throw a wolf, and not the other way around."

He had scarce finished speaking when shepherds from the valley next to theirs came running and began to inquire if their neighbours had seen two cows from their own herd—one black, they said, and the other piebald.

They proceeded to complain and lament that things had been getting out of hand lately, so many cattle had disappeared under their very eyes. And not only that. Why, only yesterday two shepherds had gone into the woods to search for sheep, and had not yet returned.

Likewise, they said, farmers from near-by villages have come to us to inquire about children. It appears that they went picking berries and were lost. But, stranger yet, yesterday at evenfall there came hurrying into our valley the wife of John the Sharpshooter, who is known as the best shot of the neighbourhood, and she told us, crying, that three days have gone by since he went chamois-chasing and he has not yet come home. No doubt about it, some mighty packs of hungry and very daring wolves must have come sneaking from the other side of the mountains.

The old herdsman listened to this tale in gloomy silence, and then said, "Nay, not wolves; they are not wolves that go ravening hereabouts; it is a werewolf and his devilish crew that are stalking about. We shall all perish pitifully, we and our herds."

A great terror came over the shepherds. They all grew silent, casting fearful glances at one another. Godfrey, however, was not a whit alarmed. He began to inquire curiously about the werewolf and his crew who frightened everybody. But the old herdsman responded thus:

"It does no good talking about it. Empty talk will avail nothing and calamity is easily invited. Be on your guard. Stay close to one another. Do not scatter and God grant that we somehow come through scatheless, for an evil creature does not like a crowd." The herdboys obeyed him and none dared leave his companions to go picking raspberries or mushrooms, while at night they huddled together like frightened sheep.

Laughter and gay talk ceased. Melancholy and fear came to reign among them. Godfrey alone did not lose his spirit, and his gay songs bore up his companions' hearts.

A few days passed in complete quiet and soon the shepherds began to take heart. Perhaps the evil was past.

First one, then another, made bold enough to stray from his companions in order to drive in a goat or to seek out some special tree for reeds.

But the wicked being did not sleep; it merely lay in wait, the better to deceive the watchful shepherds. And so it was that Jackie the Homeless, so nicknamed because he was an orphan and had no one in the world, disappeared one day without leaving a trace. He was Godfrey's dearest comrade. Dismay struck everybody, and Godfrey, despite the shepherd's interdiction, sought long and singly for his cherished companion, weeping and greatly sorrowing for him. Finally, when he returned to camp without finding the boy, he vowed in his heart he would destroy the monster. He said nothing about his decision to anyone, but constantly kept thinking of how he was going to find the werewolf.

By chance he soon found an opportunity.

One day there arrived in the valley a farmer from a far-off village in the mountains. Bowing to the herdsman, he said that he had heard of the great player from his shepherds and had come expressly to bid him to a wedding. This request did not surprise the herdsman and his boys, for, as I have said already, the fame of Godfrey's songs had spread far and wide over the region and no wedding or christening could be held without his music.

The old herdsman prided himself upon having such a player among his herders, and would gladly have given his permission. But something about this farmer did not please him; the man was shaggy like a wolf and all clothed in skins, he flashed his eyes like a wild beast, and his smile was sly and malevolent.

The old man was loath to let Godfrey go along with the stranger, therefore he took the boy aside and said, "I do not know what manner of man this is, but he has something evil in his eyes, and times are uncertain. Also, I heard my grandfather say that a werewolf can sometimes assume man's shape, the more easily to deceive and trick people. I do not like to see you go off into the mountains and wild woods with this stranger, but it would be most painful for me to deny his request. After all, he may be a very good fellow, and, as he said himself, he has come a great distance."

Godfrey was well pleased to hear these words, and thought, Grant God it is the werewolf and not a peasant from the far away mountains. I do not know yet what I am going to do, but one thing I do know: his fiendish mischief will not go unpunished.

To the herdsman he said aloud, "An old mountaineer who used to come to the valley for milk and cheese told me, too, how werewolves sometimes prowl about in human shape. But he also said they feel ill at ease in the skin of man and can easily be discovered then. For, to make themselves more comfortable, they often cast it off like an ill-suited garment, and in so doing flash a bloodshot eye or a wolf's claw. This man, however, does not act in that manner. Besides, why should he assume man's shape to lure away a little shepherd like me? Could he not, if he wished, just carry me off and do away with me, as he has done with Jackie the Homeless? He is only a common peasant, and he is hairy and ill-clad as peasants from wild mountainous regions sometimes are. It would not be right, I think, to hurt him with such suspicions and refuse his request."

"Go along with him, then, if that is your will," said the herdsman. "I will not cross you, although some uneasiness is troubling me."

Godfrey thereupon took his fiddle and, bidding

farewell to the old herdsman and the boys, set forth with the stranger.

They had not gone a long way when the stranger said to Godfrey, "The sun is scorching hot today. I must take off my cap and my sheepskin."

He removed his cap and there appeared from under it not hair, but something like a wolf's pelt.

He doffed his sheepskin and his shirt which was open on his chest revealed a body covered with hair like that of a beast.

He wiped his sweaty forehead with his hand and it was as if suddenly his hand had changed to a beast's paw.

Ho, ho, thought Godfrey, but he did not say a word.

They walked on and after a while Godfrey's companion began to complain that his shoes were greatly troubling him.

"Take them off, sir," said Godfrey, "and you will feel more comfortable."

To which the other answered, "I would take them off gladly, only I am afraid you might be frightened when you see my feet."

"Why should I be frightened?" asked Godfrey, feigning great surprise.

"Well—because my feet are not like those you are used to."

"Why?" said Godfrey, shrugging his shoulders. "Have you hoofs on your feet, or what?"

"Well, not quite hoofs. But constant walking in the mountains has given me corns and bumps which make them look like hoofs."

"I know well how the skin sometimes toughens from walking barefoot and I am not frightened by any such thing. My grandfather had such corns on his feet that they looked like two gnarled stumps. Why shouldn't yours look like hoofs? So take them off without another thought."

The stranger was greatly pleased. "You are a clever lad," he said. And sitting down on a stone he removed his shoes. Instead of toes on his feet there were hoofs just like those of devils, only so large that Godfrey was quite astonished. Yet he showed no sign of it, but smiled and said, "Hah, you are a sissy, sir. My grandfather had larger bumps and did not groan as you do."

Thus he spoke while within him great anger welled up, and rage choked him, for he now knew for certain what kind of farmer this was. And he would have leaped at the werewolf's throat then and there, but he remembered Jackie the Homeless, and thought: No, dear comrade, you shall not be unavenged. This cruel monster shall inflict no more harm on mankind. I will not be done away with for nothing. I will wait for a favourable moment and hold my anger in leash until I accomplish my design.

So they marched on all day and all night and at last they reached the devil's abode where the werewolf and his cronies, the witches and ogres, dwelt. It stood in the midst of steep and bare rocks, in a small and weirdly dismal glen. Godfrey was quite weary by the time they reached it, for the journey had been arduous, and the werewolf, once he had rid himself of his shoes which cumbered him greatly since he was unaccustomed to human footgear, had run so swiftly that Godfrey could hardly keep pace with him.

Therefore, when they came to the valley, Godfrey sat down on a stone and said, "You must let me rest awhile, sir."

"Rest yourself," replied the werewolf cheerfully. "Though it surprises me that it is only now you are feeling weary, because from here we can see the roofs of the houses, and the saying is that a horse runs faster once he sees the stable."

So they sat down together, and Godfrey peered about curiously, fixing in his mind every detail of this place.

But, to tell the truth, there was not much to see. It was a barren glen where nothing grew, and its black and hard soil suggested a big threshing floor. There was a small but deep lake almost at the far end of it, and beyond the lake there rose a hillock, huddled up against the rocks that enclosed the glen. On this very hillock the werewolf and his henchmen had put up their huts.

"What lake is that?" inquired Godfrey of the werewolf.

"That lake is called the Loch of the Drowned," returned the werewolf.

And Godfrey at once recalled what the old herdsman had told him about the lake: "The water is deep even at the short end and its mysterious whirlpools draw in the best swimmers. Nobody has ever yet come out of the lake alive."

"Well, let us go," said the werewolf, rising. "It is a

pity to waste time. Indoors you will rest and refresh yourself."

They skirted the lake and started to climb up the hill where the devils' huts stood. These did not differ much from the usual peasant huts, except that they had no windows and their walls were not whitened with lime, but were blackened with tar, since evil spirits do not like white.

Each of the huts was surrounded, as is common in the country, by a little garden. But they were queer gardens, indeed. Instead of sunflowers, cats' heads grew on tall stalks and peeped intently at passers-by, blinking their gleaming green eyes. The trees had leaves shaped like outstretched human fingers which kept curling up and straightening out, and row on row, like neatly planted cabbage-heads, grew bearded muzzles of black bucks. About the porches coiled something that looked a bit like peas and a bit like wild vine. When, however, Godfrey looked at this plant more closely he noted that its climbing stalks moved continually like a tangle of green snakes, and its flowers, shaped like long red tongues, hid and showed again, smacking greedily.

Another lad would surely have fainted with terror at such a sight, but Godfrey knew no fear. He was merely seized with loathing and great disgust but he never so much as trembled, being well aware that the werewolf was watching him intently. At last the monster stopped in front of one of the cottages and, opening the gate, entered the garden. Here he was greeted by an old dame, lean as a rod, with a thick mop of bristling hair on her head. Godfrey gazed at her, wondering what sort of freak this was, then realised that she was nothing but a plain broom prettily dressed in a skirt and bodice.

"This is the handmaid of my betrothed," said the werewolf. "She is an industrious and good girl."

And the broom began to wriggle coyly and preen herself and giggle, and veil herself with her apron, as village maidens will do.

"I am going," she said, "to give the bats a drink, because evening is falling and our cattle will wake anon."

Meanwhile the werewolf entered the cottage, so Godfrey followed him.

The room was completely dark, except for a fire that burned in the middle of it. In its red light Godfrey beheld a witch seated by the fire. Her face was as yellow as a lemon, her eyes gleamed like those of a cat and she had a long hooked nose and one green tooth which stuck out of her hideous mouth and reached down to her chin.

The werewolf at once presented Godfrey to her, saying he was the player who had been brought along for the next day's wedding.

"You must be very wayworn and hungry after so long a journey?" screeched the witch in a voice that resembled the squeak of ungreased wheels. "So be seated and eat, for the evening meal is ready."

And she brought forth some pots and cups which were like skulls of men and beasts and were filled with smoking food.

But Godfrey had no stomach for such devils' fare, wherefore he excused himself, saying that fatigue had

"I am going," she said, *"to give the bats a drink . . ."*

got the better of his hunger. He lay down in one corner of the room and pretended to fall asleep. Yet, in real truth, he did not sleep at all, but listened closely to the conversation between the witch and the werewolf.

"Why do you take such pains with this one shepherd?" said the witch to the werewolf. "Could you not just snatch him, bring him hither and force him to play, instead of going to all the trouble of putting on the guise of man?"

"Very troublesome it was indeed," answered the werewolf and, shedding the rest of his human guise, he suddenly turned into a huge wolf with shining bloodshot eyes and horse hoofs. "Phew! I can hardly breathe. Still, I could not do otherwise, for had I snatched the boy and dragged him hither, forcing him to play, he would scarcely be alive from fright and his music would not be very gay to dance to. Now, this is to be a wedding the like of which has not yet been witnessed. It isn't every day that a werewolf weds a witch."

Ho, ho, I will treat you to some wedding, thought Godfrey, still pretending to be asleep, and even snoring occasionally.

"You are right," agreed the witch. "You have contrived this wisely. But tell me, what do you propose to do with him afterward?"

The werewolf broke into laughter, exhibiting his sharp white fangs, and retorted with a grin, "Methinks a roast of the fiddler would be no worse than any other. We will eat him together with that other herdboy whom I carried away from their valley last week."

"I have been trying to fatten him up but he is still as skinny as a lath," said the witch wryly.

At these words Godfrey was overjoyed, and thought: So you are still alive, Jackie, dear. Well, please God, I will set you free, and together we shall return safe and sound to the valley.

For he had already formed his scheme to destroy the ogres, witches and the werewolf and deliver the whole region of the devil-sent plague. So he kept listening to what the witch was whispering to the werewolf.

"We are talking too loud," she said. "The boy might hear us."

"Don't be silly," replied the werewolf. "See, he is fast asleep."

And he laughed again.

"He is not so clever. He has not the slightest notion of where he is. He is a frightfully stupid boy."

Godfrey listened no longer. Now that he knew all he wanted to learn, he resolved to rest awhile. He fell asleep and slept soundly not only through that night, but through nearly all the next day as well, so weary was he from the exertion of the journey.

He was at length aroused by the preparations which the witch and the werewolf, aided by the broom, were making for the wedding.

"We shall have to clear the room," said the witch, "because once the dancing gets under way we will need every bit of space."

"That will not help much," sighed the werewolf. "The room is so small and the guests will be many."

"I know a way to avoid a crush," remarked Godfrey unexpectedly, for he had been listening closely to the conversation.

"Now, what would you suggest?" queried the were-wolf.

"If you want my advice," said Godfrey, "then do not dance indoors, but down in the valley by the lake. It is going to be a moonlit night, there will be plenty of room for dancing, and since there are no bushes or stones and the ground is level and hard, you will be more comfortable than inside. You can dance in the valley on one side of the lake while I stand on the other, on the hill, and play for you. Because of the mountains all around, the music will be echoed loud and clear throughout the valley."

"By my dear devil!" exclaimed the werewolf, who had forgotten that he was supposed to be a peasant. "By my dear devil, the lad is right."

The witch, however, was possessed of more sagacity than the werewolf, a woman being commonly shrewder than a man. So she said to Godfrey, "That is good advice about the valley. But tell me, why is it you want to stand on the other side of the lake when you play right amongst us in the valley?"

"I will explain," replied Godfrey. "You must have heard how, when I strike up a lively tune in my sweeping manner, nobody and nothing can stand still, but all must instantly start to dance and keep at it for as long as their breath holds. Well, if I should be standing in your midst, you would jostle me ever and again and hinder me from playing. And then, too, I would fain watch your dancing, and it will be much easier for me to see you from the hill than if I should stand in the middle of the crush, in the throng."

"Have it your way, then," acquiesced the witch, having dismissed her suspicions.

And straightway she ran off to invite the guests to the valley.

Ugh, 'twas a sight and something to wonder at when the guests began to assemble!

Horrible witches there were galore, those who will harm men in no time, and ogres and bogies which feed on human blood, and goblins who lead travellers astray on foggy nights. In the bright moonlight Godfrey could see clearly from his hill as the gathering paired off for dancing. They were overjoyed at having such a fiddler to play for them, for usually at devils' weddings the only music is the whistling of the wind and the croaking of toads.

Well, thought Godfrey, with God's help this shall be your last dance. And he drew the bow across the strings.

Ho! So sprightly and rousing was the music which resounded through the valley that not only the ogres, witches and goblins, led by the werewolf, began to dance; but even the brooms, who, as is well known, are in attendance upon witches, ran out of the huts and started whirling with their mistresses.

And the dancing grew ever more frenzied, ever giddier, until the dancers' breath failed, sparks began to fly before their eyes, and reason left their heads.

The witches thrust their claws into one another, and danced on.

The ogres and goblins took each other by the hand

and spun about, howling and whistling with glee so loud that the wind scurried all over the valley and the bats, startled by the wild uproar, fled in swarms from the devils huts.

The brooms lost their skirts and bodices and thrashed about right and left with such fury that from sheer impetus one and then another slashed her mistress on the pate.

In the middle was the werewolf himself, dancing, stamping his hoofs, flashing his bloodshot eyes and showing his sharp fangs.

Ha, you will not rejoice long, son of the devil, thought Godfrey, and struck the strings even more violently.

And the whole fiendish lot surged forward in one solid mass, lured onward by the irresistible call of the dance music and unmindful of the bottomless lake that separated them from the fiddler.

Perhaps one or another would have come to his senses and stopped, but the dance-drunk crowd swept him forward and carried him along.

And the fiddle kept calling from the other shore of the lake, ever louder, ever more insistently.

Onward, onward, this way, this way, the music seemed to say.

Just at the water's edge, the crowd seemed to waver, but drunk with the music and completely senseless, it plunged straight into the lake.

Thus it was that Godfrey freed the whole region of the werewolf, the ogres, witches and goblins—the whole devilish crew. In one of the huts he found Jackie the Homeless and other shepherds whom the werewolf had kept imprisoned, all of whom his music had saved from horrible death.

Great joy reigned in all the valleys and throughout the region, and the fame of Godfrey's songs, which had such power that even the devils could not resist them, spread not only over the mountains but through the length and breadth of the land until it reached the royal court.

THE WATER GHOST OF HARROWBY HALL

By JOHN KENDRICK BANGS

THE trouble with Harrowby Hall was that it was haunted, and, what was worse, the ghost did not content itself with merely appearing at the bedside of the afflicted person who saw it, but persisted in remaining there for one mortal hour before it would disappear.

It never appeared except on Christmas Eve, and then as the clock was striking twelve, in which respect alone was it lacking in that originality which in these days is a *sine qua non* of success in spectral life. The owners of Harrowby Hall had done their utmost to rid themselves of the damp and dewy lady who rose up out of the best bedroom floor at midnight, but without avail. They had tried stopping the clock, so that the ghost would not know when it was midnight; but she made her appearance just the same, with that fearful miasmatic personality of hers, and there she would stand until everything about her was thoroughly saturated.

Then the owners of Harrowby Hall calked up every crack in the floor with the very best quality of hemp, and over this were placed layers of tar and canvas; the walls were made waterproof, and the doors and windows likewise, the proprietors having conceived the notion that the unexorcised lady would find it difficult to leak into the room after these precautions had been taken; but even this did not suffice. The following Christmas Eve she appeared as promptly as before, and frightened the occupant of the room quite out of his senses by sitting down alongside of him and gazing with her cavernous blue eyes into his; and he noticed, too, that in her long, aqueously bony fingers bits of dripping seaweed were entwined, the ends hanging down, and these ends she drew across his forehead until he became like one insane. And then he swooned away, and was found unconscious in his bed the next morning by his host, simply saturated with sea-water and fright, from the combined effects of which he never recovered, dying four years later of pneumonia and nervous prostration at the age of seventy-eight.

The next year the master of Harrowby Hall decided not to have the best spare bedroom opened at all, thinking that perhaps the ghost's thirst for making

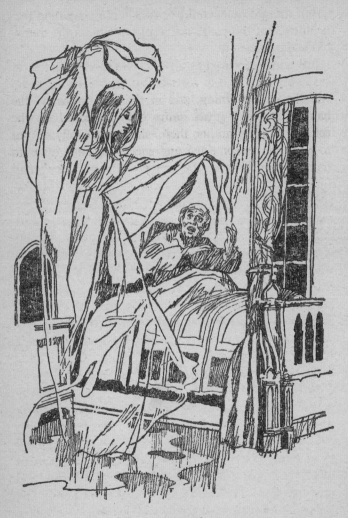

Then he swooned away, saturated with sea-water and fright

herself disagreeable would be satisfied by haunting the furniture, but the plan was as unavailing as the many that had preceded it.

The ghost appeared as usual in the room—that is, it was supposed she did, for the hangings were dripping wet the next morning, and in the parlour below the haunted room a great damp spot appeared on the ceiling. Finding no one there, she immediately set out to learn the reason why, and she chose none other to haunt than the owner of Harrowby himself. She found him in his own cosy room drinking whisky—whisky undiluted—and felicitating himself upon having foiled her ghostship, when all of a sudden the curl went out of his hair, his whisky bottle filled and overflowed, and he was himself in a condition similar to that of a man who has fallen into a water-butt. When he recovered from the shock, which was a painful one, he saw before him the lady of the cavernous eyes and seaweed fingers. The sight was so unexpected and so terrifying that he fainted, but immediately came to, because of the vast amount of water in his hair, which, trickling down over his face, restored his consciousness.

Now it so happened that the master of Harrowby was a brave man, and while he was not particularly fond of interviewing ghosts, especially such quenching ghosts as the one before him, he was not to be daunted by an apparition. He had paid the lady the compliment of fainting from the effects of his first surprise, and now that he had come to he intended to find out a few things he felt he had a right to know. He would have liked to put on a dry suit of clothes first, but the apparition declined to leave him for an instant until her hour was up, and he was forced to deny himself that pleasure. Every time he would move she would follow him, with the result that everything she came in contact with got a ducking. In an effort to warm himself up he approached the fire, an unfortunate move as it turned out, because it brought the ghost directly over the fire, which immediately was extinguished. The whisky became utterly valueless as a comforter to his chilled system, because it was by this time diluted to a proportion of ninety per cent. of water. The only thing he could do to ward off the evil effects of his encounter he did, and that was to swallow ten two-grain quinine pills, which he managed to put into his mouth before the ghost had time to interfere. Having done this, he turned with some asperity to the ghost, and said:

"Far be it from me to be impolite to a woman, madam, but I'm hanged if it wouldn't please me better if you'd stop these infernal visits of yours to this house. Go sit out on the lake, if you like that sort of thing; soak the water-butt, if you wish; but do not, I implore you, come into a gentleman's house and saturate him and his possessions in this way. It is damned disagreeable."

"Henry Hartwick Oglethorpe," said the ghost, in a gurgling voice, "you don't know what you are talking about."

"Madam," returned the unhappy householder, "I wish that remark were strictly truthful. I was talking about you. It would be shillings and pence—nay, pounds, in my pocket, madam, if I did not know you."

"That is a bit of specious nonsense," returned the ghost, throwing a quart of indignation into the face of the master of Harrowby. "It may rank high as repartee, but as a comment upon my statement, that you do not know what you are talking about, it savours of irrelevant impertinence. You do not know that I am compelled to haunt this place year after year by inexorable fate. It is no pleasure to me to enter this house, and ruin and mildew everything I touch. I never aspired to be a shower-bath, but it is my doom. Do you know who I am?"

"No, I don't," returned the master of Harrowby. "I should say you were the Lady of the Lake, or Little Sallie Waters."

"You are a witty man for your years," said the ghost.

"Well, my humour is drier than yours ever will be," returned the master.

"No doubt. I'm never dry. I am the Water Ghost of Harrowby Hall, and dryness is a quality entirely beyond my wildest hope. I have been the incumbent of this highly unpleasant office for two hundred years tonight."

"How the deuce did you ever come to get elected?" asked the master.

"Through a suicide," replied the spectre. "I am the ghost of that fair maiden whose picture hangs over the mantelpiece in the drawing-room. I should have been your great-great-great-great-great-aunt if I had lived, Henry Hartwick Oglethorpe, for I was the own sister of your great-great-great-great-great-grandfather."

"But what induced you to get this house into such a predicament?"

"I was not to blame, sir," returned the lady. "It was

my father's fault. He it was who built Harrowby Hall, and the haunted chamber was to have been mine. My father had it furnished in pink and yellow, knowing well that blue and grey formed the only combination of colour I could tolerate. He did it merely to spite me, and, with what I deem a proper spirit, I declined to live in the room; whereupon my father said I could live there or on the lawn, he didn't care which. That night I ran from the house and jumped over the cliff into the sea."

"That was rash," said the master of Harrowby. "So I've heard," returned the ghost. "If I had known what the consequences were to be I should not have jumped; but I really never realised what I was doing until after I was drowned. I had been drowned a week when a sea-nymph came to me and informed me that I was to be one of her followers forever afterwards, adding that it should be my doom to haunt Harrowby Hall for one hour every Christmas Eve throughout the rest of eternity. I was to haunt that room on such Christmas Eves as I found it inhabited; and if it should turn out not to be inhabited, I was and am to spend the allotted hour with the head of the house."

"I'll sell the place."

"That you cannot do, for it is also required of me that I shall appear as the deeds are to be delivered to any purchaser, and divulge to him the awful secret of the house."

"Do you mean to tell me that on every Christmas Eve that I don't happen to have somebody in that guest-chamber, you are going to haunt me wherever I may be, ruining my whisky, taking all the curl out of my hair, extinguishing my fire, and soaking me through to the skin?" demanded the master.

"You have stated the case, Oglethorpe. And what is more," said the water ghost, "it doesn't make the slightest difference where you are, if I find that room empty, wherever you may be I shall douse you with my spectral pres——"

Here the clock struck one, and immediately the apparition faded away. It was perhaps more of a trickle than a fade, but as a disappearance it was complete.

"By St. George and his Dragon!" ejaculated the master of Harrowby, wringing his hands. "It is guineas to hot-cross buns that next Christmas there's an occupant of the spare room, or I spend the night in a bathtub."

But the master of Harrowby would have lost his wager had there been anyone there to take him up, for when Christmas Eve came again he was in his grave, never having recovered from the cold contracted that awful night. Harrowby Hall was closed, and the heir to the estate was in London, where to him in his chambers came the same experience that his father had gone through, saving only that, being younger and stronger, he survived the shock. Everything in his rooms was ruined—his clocks were rusted in the works; a fine collection of water-colour drawings was entirely obliterated by the onslaught of the water ghost; and what was worse, the apartments below his were drenched with the water soaking through the floors, a damage for which he was compelled to pay, and which resulted in his being requested by his landlady to vacate the premises immediately.

The story of the visitation inflicted upon his family had gone abroad, and no one could be got to invite him out to any function save afternoon teas and receptions. Fathers of daughters declined to permit him to remain in their houses later than eight o'clock at night, not knowing but that some emergency might arise in the supernatural world which would require the unexpected appearance of the water ghost in this on nights other than Christmas Eve, and before the mystic hour when weary churchyards, ignoring the rules which are supposed to govern polite society, begin to yawn. Nor would maids themselves have aught to do with him, fearing the destruction by the sudden incursion of aqueous femininity of the costumes which they held most dear.

So the heir of Harrowby Hall resolved, as his ancestors for several generations before him had resolved, that something must be done. His first thought was to make one of his servants occupy the haunted room at the crucial moment; but in this he failed, because the servants themselves knew the history of that room and rebelled. None of his friends would consent to sacrifice their personal comfort to his, nor was there to be found in all England a man so poor as to be willing to occupy the doomed chamber on Christmas Eve for pay.

Then the thought came to the heir to have the fireplace in the room enlarged, so that he might evaporate the ghost at its first appearance, and he was felicitating himself upon the ingenuity of his plan,

when he remembered what his father had told him—
how that no fire could withstand the lady's extremely
contagious dampness. And then he bethought him of
steam-pipes. These, he remembered, could lie
hundreds of feet deep in water, and still retain
sufficient heat to drive the water away in vapour; and
as a result of this thought the haunted room was heated
by steam to a withering degree, and the heir for six
months attended daily the Turkish baths, so that when
Christmas Eve came he could himself withstand the
awful temperature of the room.

The scheme was only partially successful. The water
ghost appeared at the specified time, and found the heir
of Harrowby prepared; but hot as the room was, it
shortened her visit by no more than five minutes in the
hour, during which time the nervous system of the
young master was well-nigh shattered, and the room
itself was cracked and warped to an extent which
required the outlay of a large sum of money to remedy.
And worse than this, as the last drop of the water ghost
was slowly sizzling itself out on the floor, she
whispered to her would-be conqueror that his scheme
would avail him nothing, because there was still water
in great plenty where she came from, and that next
year would find her rehabilitated and as exasperatingly
saturating as ever.

It was then that the natural action of the mind, in
going from one extreme to the other, suggested to the
ingenious heir of Harrowby the means by which the
water ghost was ultimately conquered, and happiness
once more came within the grasp of the house of
Oglethorpe.

D

The heir provided himself with a warm suit of fur underclothing. Donning this with the furry side in, he placed over it a rubber garment, tightfitting, which he wore just as a woman wears a jersey. On top of this he placed another set of underclothing, this suit made of wool, and over this was a second rubber garment like the first. Upon his head he placed a light and comfortable diving helmet, and so clad, on the following Christmas Eve he awaited the coming of his tormentor.

It was a bitterly cold night that brought to a close this twenty-fourth day of December. The air outside was still, but the temperature was below zero. Within all was quiet, the servants of Harrowby Hall awaiting with beating hearts the outcome of their master's campaign against his supernatural visitor.

The master himself was lying on the bed in the haunted room, clad as has already been indicated, and then—

The clock clanged out the hour of twelve.

There was a sudden banging of doors, a blast of cold air swept through the halls, the door leading into the haunted chamber flew open, a splash was heard, and the water ghost was seen standing at the side of the heir of Harrowby, from whose outer dress there streamed rivulets of water, but whose own person deep down under the various garments he wore was as dry and as warm as he could have wished.

"Ha!" said the young master of Harrowby. "I'm glad to see you."

"You are the most original man I've met, if that is

true," returned the ghost. "May I ask where did you get that hat?"

"Certainly, madam," returned the master, courteously. "It is a little portable observatory I had made for just such emergencies as this. But, tell me, is it true that you are doomed to follow me about for one mortal hour—to stand where I stand, to sit where I sit?"

"That is my delectable fate," returned the lady.

"We'll go out on the lake," said the master, starting up.

"You can't get rid of me that way," returned the ghost. "The water won't swallow me up; in fact, it will just add to my present bulk."

"Nevertheless," said the master, firmly, "we will go out on the lake."

"But my dear sir," returned the ghost, with a pale reluctance, "it is fearfully cold out there. You will be frozen hard before you've been out ten minutes."

"Oh, no, I'll not," replied the master. "I am very warmly dressed. Come!" This last in a tone of command that made the ghost ripple.

And they started.

They had not gone far before the water ghost showed signs of distress.

"You walk too slowly," she said. "I am nearly frozen. My knees are so stiff now I can hardly move. I beseech you to accelerate your step."

"I should like to oblige a lady," returned the master, courteously, "but my clothes are rather heavy, and a hundred yards an hour is about my speed. Indeed, I think we would better sit down here on this snowdrift, and talk matters over."

"Do not! Do not do so, I beg!" cried the ghost. "Let me move on. I feel myself growing rigid as it is. If we stop here, I shall be frozen stiff."

"That, madam," said the master slowly, and seating himself on an ice-cake—"that is why I have brought you here. We have been on this spot just ten minutes; we have fifty more. Take your time about it, madam, but freeze, that is all I ask of you."

"I cannot move my right leg now," cried the ghost, in despair, "and my overskirt is a solid sheet of ice. Oh, good, kind Mr. Oglethorpe, light a fire, and let me go free from these icy fetters."

"Never, madam. It cannot be. I have you at last."

"Alas!" cried the ghost, a tear trickling down her frozen cheek. "Help me, I beg. I congeal!"

"Congeal, madam, congeal!" returned Oglethorpe, coldly. "You have drenched me and mine for two hundred and three years, madam. Tonight, you have had your last drench."

"Ah, but I shall thaw out again, and then you'll see. Instead of the comfortably tepid, genial ghost I have been in my past, sir, I shall be iced-water," cried the lady, threateningly.

"No, you won't either," returned Oglethorpe; "for when you are frozen quite stiff, I shall send you to a cold-storage warehouse, and there shall you remain an icy work of art forever more."

"But warehouses burn."

"So they do, but this warehouse cannot burn. It is made of asbestos and surrounding it are fireproofed walls, and within those walls the temperature is now and shall forever be 416 degrees below the zero point;

low enough to make an icicle of any flame in this world—or the next," the master added, with an ill-suppressed chuckle.

"For the last time let me beseech you. I would go on my knees to you, Oglethorpe, were they not already frozen. I beg of you do not doo—"

Here even the words froze on the water ghost's lips and the clock struck one. There was a momentary tremor throughout the ice-bound form, and the moon, coming out from behind a cloud, shone down on the rigid figure of a beautiful woman sculptured in clear, transparent ice. There stood the ghost of Harrowby Hall, conquered by the cold, a prisoner for all time.

The heir of Harrowby had won at last, and today in a large storage house in London stands the frigid form of one who will never again flood the house of Oglethorpe with woe and sea-water.

As for the heir of Harrowby, his success in coping with a ghost has made him famous, a fame that still lingers about him, although his victory took place some twenty years ago; and so far from being unpopular with the fair sex, as he was when we first knew him, he has not only been married twice, but is to lead a third bride to the altar before the year is out.

THE RED ROOM

By H. G. WELLS

"I CAN assure you," said I, "that it will take a very tangible ghost to frighten me." And I stood up before the fire with my glass in my hand.

"It is your own choosing," said the man with the withered arm, and glanced at me askance.

"Eight-and-twenty years," said I, "I have lived, and never a ghost have I seen as yet."

The old woman sat staring hard into the fire, her pale eyes wide open. "Ay," she broke in; "and eight-and-twenty years you have lived and never seen the likes of this house, I reckon. There's a many things to see, when one's still but eight-and-twenty." She swayed her head slowly from side to side. "A many things to see and sorrow for."

I half suspected the old people were trying to enhance the spiritual terrors of their house by their droning insistence. I put down my empty glass on the table and looked about the room, and caught a glimpse of myself, abbreviated and broadened to an impossible sturdiness, in the queer old mirror at the end of the room. "Well," I said, "if I see anything tonight, I shall be so much the wiser. For I come to the business with an open mind."

"It's your own choosing," said the man with the withered arm once more.

I heard the sound of a stick and a shambling step on the flags in the passage outside, and the door creaked on its hinges as a second old man entered, more bent, more wrinkled, more aged even than the first. He supported himself by a single crutch, his eyes were covered by a shade, and his lower lip, half-averted, hung pale and pink from his decaying yellow teeth. He made straight for an arm-chair on the opposite side of the table, sat down clumsily, and began to cough. The man with the withered arm gave this newcomer a short glance of positive dislike; the old woman took no notice of his arrival, but remained with her eyes fixed steadily on the fire.

"I said—it's your own choosing," said the man with the withered arm, when the coughing had ceased for a while.

"It's my own choosing," I answered.

The man with the shade became aware of my presence for the first time, and threw his head back for a moment and sideways, to see me. I caught a momentary glimpse of his eyes, small and bright and inflamed. Then he began to cough and splutter again.

"Why don't you drink?" said the man with the withered arm, pushing the beer towards him. The man with the shade poured out a glassful with a shaky arm that splashed half as much again on the deal table. A monstrous shadow of him crouched upon the wall and mocked his action as he poured and drank. I must confess I had scarce expected these grotesque custodians. There is to my mind something inhuman in senility, something crouching and atavistic; the human qualities seem to drop from old people insensibly day by day. The three of them made me feel uncomfortable, with their gaunt silences, their bent carriage, their evident unfriendliness to me and to one another.

"If," said I, "you will show me to this haunted room of yours, I will make myself comfortable there."

The old man with the cough jerked his head back so suddenly that it startled me, and shot another glance of his red eyes at me from under the shade; but no one answered me. I waited a minute, glancing from one to the other.

"If," I said a little louder, "if you will show me to this haunted room of yours, I will relieve you from the task of entertaining me."

"There's a candle on the slab outside the door," said the man with the withered arm, looking at my feet as he addressed me. "But if you go to the red room tonight——"

("This night of all nights!" said the old woman.)

"You go alone."

"Very well," I answered. "And which way do I go?"

"You go along the passage for a bit," said he, "until you come to a door, and through that is a spiral staircase, and half-way up that is a landing and another door covered with baize. Go through that and down the long corridor to the end, and the red room is on your left up the steps."

"Have I got that right?" I said, and repeated his directions. He corrected me in one particular.

"And are you really going?" said the man with the

shade, looking at me again for the third time, with that queer, unnatural tilting of the face.

("This night of all nights!" said the old woman.)

"It is what I came for," I said, and moved towards the door. As I did so, the old man with the shade rose and staggered round the table, so as to be closer to the others and to the fire. At the door I turned and looked at them, and saw they were all close together, dark against the firelight, staring at me over their shoulders, with an intent expression on their ancient faces.

"Goodnight," I said, setting the door open.

"It's your own choosing," said the man with the withered arm.

I left the door wide open until the candle was well alight, and then I shut them in and walked down the chilly, echoing passage.

I must confess that the oddness of these three old pensioners in whose charge her ladyship had left the castle, and the deep-toned, old-fashioned furniture of the housekeeper's room in which they foregathered, affected me in spite of my efforts to keep myself at a matter-of-fact phase. They seemed to belong to another age, an older age, an age when things spiritual were different from this of ours, less certain; an age when omens and witches were credible, and ghosts beyond denying. Their very existence was spectral; the cut of their clothing, fashions born in dead brains. The ornaments and conveniences of the room about them were ghostly—the thoughts of vanished men, which still haunted rather than participated in the world of today. But with an effort I sent such thoughts to the right-about. The long, draughty subterranean passage was chilly and dusty, and my candle flared and made the shadows cower and quiver. The echoes rang up and down the spiral staircase, and a shadow came sweeping up after me, and one fled before me into the darkness overhead. I came to the landing and stopped there for a moment, listening to a rustling that I fancied I heard; then, satisfied of the absolute silence, I pushed open the baize-covered door and stood in the corridor.

The effect was scarcely what I expected, for the moonlight coming in by the great window on the grand staircase picked out everything in vivid black shadow or silvery illumination. Everything was in its place; the house might have been deserted on the yesterday instead of eighteen months ago. There were candles in the sockets of the sconces, and whatever dust had gathered on the carpets or upon the polished flooring was distributed so evenly as to be invisible in the moonlight. I was about to advance, and stopped abruptly. A bronze group stood upon the landing, hidden from me by the corner of the wall, but its shadow fell with marvellous distinctness upon the white panelling and gave me the impression of some one crouching to waylay me. I stood rigid for half a minute perhaps. Then, with my hand in the pocket that held my revolver, I advanced, only to discover a Ganymede and Eagle glistening in the moonlight. That incident for a time restored my nerve, and a porcelain Chinaman on a buhl table, whose head rocked silently as I passed him, scarcely startled me.

The door to the red room and the steps up to it were in a shadowy corner. I moved my candle from side to side, in order to see clearly the nature of the recess in which I stood before opening the door. Here it was, thought I, that my predecessor was found, and the memory of that story gave me a sudden twinge of apprehension. I glanced over my shoulder at the Ganymede in the moonlight, and opened the door of the red room rather hastily, with my face half-turned to the pallid silence of the landing.

I entered, closed the door behind me at once, turned the key I found in the lock within, and stood with the candle held aloft, surveying the scene of my vigil, the great red room of Lorraine Castle, in which the young duke had died. Or, rather, in which he had begun his dying, for he had opened the door and fallen headlong down the steps I had just ascended. That had been the end of his vigil, of his gallant attempt to conquer the ghostly tradition of the place, and never, I thought, had apoplexy better served the ends of superstition. And there were other and older stories that clung to the room, back to the half-credible beginning of it all, the tale of a timid wife and the tragic end that came to her husband's jest of frightening her. And looking around that large sombre room, with its shadowy window bays, its recesses and alcoves, one could well understand the legends that had sprouted in its black corners, its germinating darkness. My candle was a little tongue of light in its vastness, that failed to pierce the opposite end of the room, and left an ocean of mystery and suggestion beyond its island of light.

I resolved to make a systematic examination of the place at once, and dispel the fanciful suggestions of its obscurity before they obtained a hold upon me. After satisfying myself of the fastening of the door, I began to walk about the room, peering round each article of furniture, tucking up the valances of the bed, and opening its curtains wide. I pulled up the blinds and examined the fastenings of the several windows before closing the shutters, leant forward and looked up the blackness of the wide chimney, and tapped the dark oak panelling for any secret opening. There were two big mirrors in the room, each with a pair of sconces bearing candles, and on the mantelshelf, too, were more candles in china candlesticks. All these I lit one after the other. The fire was laid, an unexpected consideration from the old housekeeper—and I lit it, to keep down any disposition to shiver, and when it was burning well, I stood round with my back to it and regarded the room again. I had pulled up a chintz-covered armchair and a table, to form a kind of barricade before me, and on this lay my revolver ready to hand. My precise examination had done me good, but I still found the remoter darkness of the place, and its perfect stillness, too stimulating for the imagination. The echoing of the stir and crackling of the fire was no sort of comfort to me. The shadow in the alcove at the end in particular had that undefinable quality of a presence, that odd suggestion of a lurking, living thing, that comes so easily in silence and solitude. At last, to reassure myself, I walked with a candle into it, and satisfied myself that there was nothing tangible there. I stood that candle upon the floor of the alcove, and left it in that position.

By this time I was in a state of considerable nervous tension, although to my reason there was no adequate cause for the condition. My mind, however, was perfectly clear. I postulated quite unreservedly that nothing supernatural could happen, and to pass the time I began to string some rhymes together, Ingoldsby fashion, of the original legend of the place. A few I spoke aloud, but the echoes were not pleasant. For the same reason I also abandoned, after a time, a conversation with myself upon the impossibility of ghosts and haunting. My mind reverted to the three old and distorted people downstairs, and I tried to keep it upon that topic. The sombre reds and blacks of the room troubled me; even with seven candles the place was merely dim. The one in the alcove flared in a draught, and the fire-flickering kept the shadows and penumbra perpetually shifting and stirring. Casting about for a remedy, I recalled the candles I had seen in the passage, and, with a slight effort, walked out into the moonlight, carrying a candle and leaving the door open, and presently returned with as many as ten. These I put in various knick-knacks of china with which the room was sparsely adorned, lit and placed where the shadows had lain deepest, some on the floor, some in the window recesses, until at last my seventeen candles were so arranged that not an inch of the room but had the direct light of at least one of them. It occurred to me that when the ghost came, I could warn him not to trip over them. The room was now quite brightly illuminated. There was something very cheery and reassuring in these little streaming flames, and snuffing them gave me an occupation, and afforded a helpful sense of the passage of time.

Even with that, however, the brooding expectation

of the vigil weighed heavily upon me. It was after midnight that the candle in the alcove suddenly went out, and the black shadow sprang back to its place there. I did not see the candle go out; I simply turned and saw that the darkness was there, as one might start and see the unexpected presence of a stranger. "By Jove!" said I aloud; "that draught's a strong one!" and taking the matches from the table, I walked across the room in a leisurely manner to re-light the corner again. My first match would not strike, and as I succeeded with the second, something seemed to blink on the wall before me. I turned my head involuntarily, and saw that the two candles on the little table by the fireplace were extinguished. I rose at once to my feet.

"Odd!" I said. "Did I do that myself in a flash of absent-mindedness?"

I walked back, re-lit one, and as I did so, I saw the candle in the right sconce of one of the mirrors wink and go right out, and almost immediately its companion followed it. There was no mistake about it. The flame vanished, as if the wicks had been suddenly nipped between a finger and a thumb, leaving the wick neither glowing nor smoking, but black. While I stood gaping, the candle at the foot of the bed went out, and the shadows seemed to take another step towards me.

"This won't do!" said I, and first one and then another candle on the mantelshelf followed.

"What's up?" I cried, with a queer high note getting into my voice somehow. At that the candle on the wardrobe went out, and the one I had re-lit in the alcove followed.

"Steady on!" I said. "These candles are wanted,"

speaking with a half-hysterical facetiousness, and scratching away at a match the while for the mantel candlesticks. My hands trembled so much that twice I missed the rough paper of the matchbox. As the mantel emerged from darkness again, two candles in the remoter end of the window were eclipsed. But with the same match I also re-lit the larger mirror candles, and those on the floor near the doorway, so that for the moment I seemed to gain on the extinctions. But then in a volley there vanished four lights at once in different corners of the room, and I struck another match in quivering haste, and stood hesitating whither to take it.

As I stood undecided, an invisible hand seemed to sweep out the two candles on the table. With a cry of terror, I dashed at the alcove, then into the corner, and then into the window, re-lighting three, as two more vanished by the fireplace; then, perceiving a better way, I dropped the matches on the iron-bound deedbox in the corner, and caught up the bedroom candle-stick. With this I avoided the delay of striking matches; but for all that the steady process of extinction went on, and the shadows I feared and fought against returned, and crept in upon me, first a step gained on this side of me and then on that. It was like a ragged storm-cloud sweeping out the stars. Now and then one returned for a minute, and was lost again. I was now almost frantic with the horror of the coming darkness, and my self-possession deserted me. I leaped panting and dishevelled from candle to candle in a vain struggle against that remorseless advance.

I bruised myself on the thigh against the table, I sent

111

a chair headlong, I stumbled and fell and whisked the cloth from the table in my fall. My candle rolled away from me, and I snatched another as I rose. Abruptly this was blown out, as I swung it off the table by the wind of my sudden movement, and immediately the two remaining candles followed. But there was light still in the room, a red light that staved off the shadows from me. The fire! Of course I could still thrust my candle between the bars and re-light it!

I turned to where the flames were still dancing between the glowing coals, and splashing red reflections upon the furniture, made two steps towards the grate, and incontinently the flames dwindled and vanished, the glow vanished, the reflections rushed together and vanished, and as I thrust the candle between the bars darkness close upon me like the shutting of an eye, wrapped about me in a stifling embrace, sealed my vision, and crushed the last vestiges of reason from my brain. The candle fell from my hand. I flung out my arms in a vain effort to thrust that ponderous blackness away from me, and, lifting up my voice, screamed with all my might—once, twice, thrice. Then I think I must have staggered to my feet. I know I thought suddenly of the moonlit corridor, and, with my head bowed and my arms over my face, made a run for the door.

But I had forgotten the exact position of the door, and struck myself heavily against the corner of the bed. I staggered back, turned, and was either struck or struck myself against some other bulky furniture. I have a vague memory of battering myself thus, to and fro in the darkness, of a cramped struggle, and of my own wild crying as I darted to and fro, of a heavy blow at last upon my forehead, a horrible sensation of falling that lasted an age, of my last frantic effort to keep my footing, and then I remember no more.

I opened my eyes in daylight. My head was roughly bandaged, and the man with the withered arm was watching my face. I looked about me, trying to remember what had happened, and for a space I could not recollect. I rolled my eyes into the corner, and saw the old woman, no longer abstracted, pouring out some drops of medicine from a little blue phial into a glass. "Where am I?" I asked; "I seem to remember you, and yet I cannot remember who you are."

They told me then, and I heard of the haunted Red Room as one who hears a tale. "We found you at dawn," said he, "and there was blood on your forehead and lips."

It was very slowly I recovered my memory of my experience. "You believe now," said the old man, "that the room is haunted?" He spoke no longer as one who greets an intruder, but as one who grieves for a broken friend.

"Yes," said I; "the room is haunted."

"And you have seen it. And we, who have lived here all our lives, have never set eyes upon it. Because we have never dared . . . Tell us, is it truly the old earl who——"

"No," said I; "it is not."

"I told you so," said the old lady, with the glass in her hand. "It is his poor young countess who was frightened——"

"It is not," I said. "There is neither ghost or earl

113

nor ghost of countess in that room, there is no ghost there at all; but worse, far worse——"

"Well?" they said.

"The worst of all the things that haunt poor mortal man," said I; "and that is, in all its nakedness—*Fear!* Fear that will not have light nor sound, that will not bear with reason, that deafens and darkens and overwhelms. It followed me through the corridor, it fought against me in the room——"

I stopped abruptly. There was an interval of silence. My hand went up to my bandages.

Then the man with the shade sighed and spoke. "That is it," said he. "I knew that was it. A power of darkness. To put such a curse upon a woman! It lurks there always. You can feel it even in the daytime, even of a bright summer's day, in the hangings, in the curtains, keeping behind you however you face about. In the dusk it creeps along the corridor and follows you, so that you dare not turn. There is Fear in that room of hers—black Fear, and there will be—so long as this house of sin endures."

SPOOKS OF THE VALLEY

By Louis C. Jones

THE boys were working intently on the tail assembly of the model transport plane. Joe was holding the small piece of balsa wood neatly in place while Pete carefully spread the glue along the crevice. It was well after bedtime, for Pete's folks, when they went out, had told the boys to go upstairs at eight-thirty, and now the clock was striking nine. But the problem of the tail was a tough one and could hardly be left for tomorrow. Besides, Joe didn't come to spend the night very often. When they heard the first step on the top stair they hardly noticed it. At the second step Pete spoke up sharply, but without raising his eyes from their task.

"Sis, you get on back to bed. You know what Mom told you. You're gonna get in trouble."

The footsteps kept coming slowly down the stairs just as he rather expected they would, young sisters being what they are. It wasn't the weight on the steps that made him turn, for that was light enough, but Sister never came down a pair of stairs slowly in her

115

life. And if it wasn't Carol, who was it? This took a few seconds, especially since Pete's mind really wasn't on the stairs but on the model. It wasn't until Joe said, "Okay now," and put the tube of glue down, that Pete turned around.

Never before had he seen the man who stood there—tall and gaunt, with tanned, knotty hands and a weary stoop to his shoulders. His clothes were ragged and strangely out of date. Pete wasn't scared, just surprised. You couldn't really be scared of a face like this man's. It was an interesting face, with kind, sad lines around the mouth and the grey eyes. It looked like a face that had seen a lot of things, and the expression of the eyes made you ponder. Pete was still gaping when Joe spoke.

"Well, hello, George! So you really came up, did you?"

"Yeah," the man said, "I figured you two would be alone tonight so I kind of hung around outside until Pete's folks went away. Then I just wandered in and looked around until I found you."

"Who is this guy?" Pete asked, still surprised not to see his sister.

"This is George, Pete. I told you about George. I told you all about him on the 'bus the other day."

"You mean," said Pete, "that you weren't kidding? I thought you made all that up."

"Pete, you know I never make things up. I'm not always having crazy ideas like you. George, this is Pete."

"Pete, I'm glad to meet you. I'm mighty glad to

meet you, 'cause I think you can help me," said George in a hopeful voice.

"Gee, I'd like to help you, George," said Pete. "That is—I guess I would. Are you really—I mean, is it like Joe told me? Aren't you——"

"Well, now, Pete. I don't know. I don't know just what Joe told you. If he told you how I used to peddle tin all through this section, and how this was the last farm I ever stopped at, and how I'm needing your help now—I guess he told you right. You see, Pete, the way it is, I can't rest. I got this thing on my mind all the time, and that way you don't get any rest. People ought not to do things like that, and it was a long time ago, of course, and somebody who lives here now has got to make it right. I tried to get to your old man, and I tried to get to your mom, but they couldn't hear me and they couldn't see me. I figured maybe you were the only one I could talk to."

"Well, gee, George, I guess we can help you if it isn't too hard to do. Do we have to do it tonight?"

"Well," said George, "it would be kind of nice if you could. This business is sort of delicate, but there's a good moon out, and though I don't want to get you in trouble, it will be quite a spell before your folks get back."

He seemed so earnest and hopeful about it that the boys felt they really had to help.

"How do we start?" asked Joe.

"All you got to do, boys, is this. You go out to that big woodpile—the old woodpile in the back of the barn——"

"We haven't touched that woodpile since we moved

here four years ago," broke in Pete. "Pop cut down so many trees and sawed 'em up for firewood that we just haven't had to use that wood out behind the barn."

"I know that, son," said George, "and nobody else has touched that woodpile. Some of that wood's been there ten years, and before that they kept putting fresh wood on every winter, so that nobody's been down to the bottom of that pile since 1853. But all I want you boys to do is go down to the far end of that pile and tear it to pieces. Get right down to the ground and then start digging until you come to the place where my tin is buried. Won't be much now—just a few pieces of rust—but then you'll know you're in the right spot and you keep digging down below that. Then you come to the important thing . . ."

Pete was listening intently to every word George said, and then suddenly he realised that something weird and wonderful was happening. George was disappearing. It was not that he was going away—it's just that when he finished the sentence, he wasn't there. First there had been three of them and now there were only two.

"Whillikers!" said Pete, "I'd somehow forgotten all about his being dead."

Pete ran upstairs and looked in to see if his brother and sister were asleep. They certainly were, all right. Carol was snoring happily to herself and Davie was hugging his little old bear for dear life. Then Pete got some mittens and a couple of sweaters, because the October air was cold. Both boys walked out the back door and down behind the barn where the full moon shone cold and clear on the old woodpile, six feet high and four cord wide.

The wood was dry and light, and they started at the top and threw it off the cord so it fell every which way in the grass. After a little bit Joe was puffing and Pete had stopped to sit down and rest himself.

"This isn't easy!" Pete said slowly.

"But we gotta do it. I promised George that first night I met him."

"How'd you get mixed up in this, Joe?"

"It was like I told you—that calf Pa gave me got her foot caught in a stanchion. I heard her bellowing and went down to the barn along about nine o'clock to get it loose. Coming back, I saw lights in the old Staats house. I knew the Staatses weren't there, and down the little road between our house and theirs I saw George pacing up and down. 'Course I didn't know he was a— I mean, I thought he was just a man. I didn't see any reason to be scared of him, so I says, 'Hello,' and he says, 'Hello, you're Joe, aren't you?' And I says, 'Yep, I'm Joe. I never saw you around before.' So he says, 'No, but I have been watching you. Sometimes I see you down here and sometimes I see you visitin' up to your friend Pete's.' So I says, 'Do you know Pete?' And he says, 'Nope, but I wish I did. He's about the only one could really help me.' 'What's the matter?' I says to him, and he comes back with, 'What I got, the trouble with me, is hard to say. I'm not like you. I been dead, you know, 'most a hundred years.' Well, when he said it like that, Pete, I could have jumped. We see 'em around, of course. Especially at night around the Staats place where they like to come—they

119

have parties down there sometimes. But I never talked to one, 'specially not about being a ghost. You might say he was just matter of fact about it. Like I'd say, 'I'm a boy.' That's the way he said it."

Pete was quiet for a minute. Then he said, "I think I would have been scared."

"You weren't scared tonight when George came in. The dead seem so natural, don't they?"

There was a long silence then. Somewhere a lone bird chirped just a little. Mr. Ostrander's cow complained in the next field. It was awful quiet. After a bit the boys got up and began pulling down the pile again. They were halfway done now. Their hands were getting tired and they were slowing down. After a while they took another spell of sitting, and Pete said, "When did he tell you, exactly, about this?"

"It was that same night after I had gone to bed. George came into the room and sat down and told me. It seems that the year this all happened, he was carrying around all the money he had saved up for five years. He was gonna open a little store down in Hudson or Catskill or someplace. He didn't know anybody to take care of the money for him and he didn't trust banks, so he had it all wadded up in big bills in his pants' pocket. It came along toward winter and he had pretty well sold out everything he had. When he started out he had had a horse and cart piled up with tins—pots, pans, and stuff. He was down to four or five pans, and the week before he had had a chance to sell his horse and cart for a good price. He wasn't going to need them when he opened up his store so he grabbed the chance and sold out.

"Well, he came to your house along about dusk one night and some new folks had bought the place. There was a man and a woman with the meanest hired man he had ever seen in his life—a great burly fellow with hairy arms, and his teeth stuck out of the corners like a dog. George asked them could he stay there that night. All he wanted was a place to lay his blanket. They said he could sleep on the floor up in the hired man's room."

"That must be my room now, isn't it?" asked Pete, trying to get a word in edgewise.

"That's the way I figure it. Anyway, this hired man didn't like the idea, was mighty crabby about it.

"When they were getting undressed George suddenly sneezed and he pulled his handkerchief out and this big wad of bills came with it. The fellow saw the bills and didn't say much, but after George had got to sleep he had this dream about not being able to breathe. Just as he was waking up, he opened his eyes, and the moonlight was coming right on the face of this great big fellow who was choking the very life out of him. Well, sir, he was dead before he knew it.

"Then he stayed around while the hired man picked up his body and very carefully came down those back stairs from your bedroom, down through the kitchen, out in back where this woodpile is—right here where we're sitting. And George says first he took the wood down just like we've done now. Then he dug a grave under where the woodpile had been, putting the dirt into bushel baskets. Then he buried George and put the tin that was left on top, covered it over with dirt and piled up the wood again the way it had been.

121

Then he took the dirt that was left and spread it all over the garden. The next morning he just told the folks that the tin man had left at the crack of dawn."

Maybe it was the cold, maybe it was a stray owl that was hooting out in the pine trees, maybe it was the funny shadows that passed over the moon—but Pete sat on the woodpile shivering.

"Look, Joe, what do you say we do this some other time? I'm not so sure I want to get mixed up in this."

"You wouldn't let me down now, would you?" came a third voice from the darkness. And there was George, standing there looking at him, sad as he could be.

"Pete, my boy, you don't know what it is to have your body buried off in a forsaken spot like the bottom of a woodpile. A man likes to feel he's buried with people. You don't have to have a fancy monument, but the place for a dead man is in a cemetery, and I can't rest like a man ought to until my bones are taken out of this place and put where they belong."

"What about this hired man, George?" Pete's voice was small and sort of sick sounding.

"Oh, him!" George answered. "It didn't take me long to handle him. Two days after he'd killed me, he ran away from here, and I followed him. He went out and walked along the railroad track. About two miles from here, just beyond Van Hoesen, a train came pounding down the line and he stepped off the track, but not quite far enough. I gave him a little shove and that was the end of him. It's a bad thing to have a dead man mad at you. It's a worse thing to steal a dead man's money—'specially if it's every cent he's saved for six hard years. I tell you, Pete, I never hurt a single soul as long as I was alive, but he was a bummer and I fixed him in my own time."

Pete's worry wasn't quite caught up.

"He isn't still around by any chance?" he asked apprehensively.

"I never saw him," said George. "He never comes down with the others to the Staats place when we have our meetings. No, I never saw him again."

After a pause, he said, "Now what do you say, boys —let's get this done. There isn't much time, you know, before your folks get back."

They worked hard for a few minutes and then another few and before they knew it, sure enough, they were down to the bare ground. Pete disappeared and came back with a spade and a shovel—and while George watched, they dug.

Now this was really hard work and they began to sweat and pant. Just as it seemed an endless job, there was a scraping noise and something more than stone was in the dirt. When they picked it up, it was the handle of a skillet. George remembered it.

"A first-rate piece of merchandise." That's what he said of it. But now there was just a handle—the rest had rusted away. But there were other pieces of metal and the boys kept digging.

"Take it easy now. I think you're getting close," George cautioned. And, sure enough, pretty soon a bone like the upper part of a man's arm lay in the dirt. Pete got a bushel basket and put it in very gently. Joe kept digging and soon they found another. And another. Finally the skull—full of dirt and worms, but clean as it could be once you knocked the soil away. As George watched them carefully putting each piece in the basket, he spoke softly:

"You're very kind to me, boys. Very thoughtful young men you are."

Pretty soon Joe asked him, "Have we got it all there now? Seems like we've picked a couple of hundred bones out of the dirt. They're hard to see, you know, even in this moonlight."

"I think there's a hand missing, boys. It feels to me that way. I don't feel you've got my other hand yet."

"Do you have any idea where it would be?" Joe asked.

"Try right there," said George and pointed.

They dug a little more and pretty soon they found the bones as though they had been all clenched together and the boys picked them up in a couple of handfuls. They took the basket and hid it in the haymow in the barn and then came back to fill the hole in just as fast as they could move. Then they piled up the wood again as best they could. Fortunately, that was a part of the farm where almost no one ever came, so its chance of being seen was pretty small. The midnight express went screaming down the B. & A. tracks a mile away about the time the boys had piled the last stick in place.

The past half hour Pete had been getting nervous because he knew that it was almost time for his folks to be coming home and if he weren't in bed asleep, they'd make an awful squawk. And if they knew what he had been up to, there was no telling what would happen.

Every time a car light came up the road he would look over his shoulder at it.

"What's the matter, Pete?" George asked. "You ain't still worrying about that hired man, are you?"

"No, I was more worried about my old man than your hired man. It's about time they're comin' home."

"Oh, them," said George, "don't worry about them. I had one of my friends in town stick a nail in your father's tyre, just so he wouldn't hurry home too fast. I don't think he'll be here for a spell yet. And, boys, I want to say how grateful I am to you, but there's one other little matter. Where are you going to rebury me?"

"Well," said Joe, "I thought we'd take you down to that old burying ground outside the Staats place. It would be near the house down there and handy for your parties."

"That's fine," said George, "that's fine. Now, when?" There was persistence in his tone.

"Well," said Pete, "I'm going down to Joe's to spend Saturday night and if you wouldn't mind my putting the bones in a bag, I could take them down on my bike when I go. Then we could fix it up for you sometime over the weekend."

"Boys, that's just fine. That's just fine. Down there I'll be real happy. If there's anything I can ever do for you, you let me know."

"It's okay," said Joe, "we're glad to help you out."

"Would you—sometime——" broke off Pete, not knowing how to go on.

"What, son? Anything at all."

"Saturday, mebbe, would you tell us more about—

about being dead? And about some of the ghosts—the other ghosts, I mean."

"Why not? I'll tell you all I know—and what I don't know ain't worth knowin'." And for the first time George grinned at them. "You bury me the way I ought to be, and then Saturday we'll get together. How's that?" They were about to answer him, but George had disappeared once more.

Right after breakfast on Saturday Pete fed the chickens and before his mother quite realised it, he was off on his bike for Joe's house. In the basket on his handle bars was a grain bag, neatly folded. It made an irregular package but it weighed so little that he barely realised it was there. Best of all, he had been able to hide it up by the trees at the north end of his farm the night before, so that in the morning he could pick it up without the endless questions that grown-ups are forever asking a boy.

Pete lived two miles or more back from the Hudson, high above the river. He pedalled along rapidly, finally coming to the airport road which dropped down to the river road, past Citizen Genet's old house. As he swung down the hill, bracing himself against the pull of the brakes, he caught the long view of the river with Albany to the right, its hillside towers against the sky, then far to the left the Castleton Bridge carrying the freight trains over the cut-off. When he reached the river road he turned left for a mile, then took a side road leading to the river.

Joe lived on an island, separated from the mainland by a longish bridge. Before the river was deepened it was more of an island, but even now during the spring floods sometimes they were cut off from the mainland. As Pete pumped his bike up over the New York Central tracks he could see the farm buildings ahead of him, the ancient barns and the farmhouse made over and modernised but really the same house that had been there for nearly two centuries.

"Hi, Joeyeeee." It made a crazy sound as Pete called it.

But back from the barn came "Hiyi, Pete." And Joe came running.

Five minutes later the two boys were walking rapidly down the little grass-covered wagon track that led to the south end of the island and the old Staats house with its aged cemetery. Each carried a shovel over his shoulder and the bag of bones between them, not because it was heavy, but to share the responsibility.

"George was here last night," said Joe casually.

"Yeah?"

"He told me just where he wants them buried. Over near old Jakob Staats in the far corner. Says the old man was a good customer of his and a good friend. And besides, no one will notice a new grave there."

By now they had come to the gateway of the little family burying ground with its headstones that told the story of a family that are said to have come to the Hudson Valley sometime before 1640 and had always lived on that land. The boys found Jakob's grave off in its far corner, just as George had told Joe they would, and they began to dig. It was easy going, for the soil was sandy.

"How deep do you think we ought to go?" Pete asked when they were down a couple of feet.

"Six feet is the customary depth," said a voice that made them jump halfway out of their skins.

"Holy Moses, George! I wish you wouldn't scare us so," scolded Joe.

"I thought you had to wait till night, George. Can you come around any—Hey, George, where are you?" Pete was bewildered, for, close as the voice was, there was no George to be seen.

"Pete, my friend," the old man said, "your notions about us dead are way out of date. Any time of day or night, that's us. Sometimes we 'show' and sometimes we don't; that's up to us. Look!"

And sure enough, after a second or two there he was, as real as a tree. Then he roared with laughter, slapping his thigh, as he saw the look on the boys' faces. "There are a lot of silly notions going around about us. Chain rattling, for instance. Almost nobody, that is, no *dead* body, rattles chains, that I know of. And water! They tell you we can't cross water. Fiddle-faddle! How would the whole bunch of us get to an *island* for our meetings and parties, down here at the Staats house, if we couldn't cross water? As a matter of fact, we can do almost anything we could when we were alive. More things, really. Couldn't disappear when I was alive." And with that he wasn't there any more, just the sound of his laugh as the boys stared at the air where he had been.

"George is feeling a lot more cheerful, isn't he?" Pete observed.

"Told me he felt like a new spirit since we dug him up," Joe said. "He's much more fun than he was."

128

They dug for a spell, thinking over what they had heard, thinking, too, about the fact that George was there by them, watching. They figured the hole didn't have to be very long or wide. First one would get down and work awhile, then the other. They did a lot of resting, but not even Joe was talking much. The deeper they went, the harder going it was. When Pete was waist-deep he said, "George, that isn't six feet, but how about it? Don't you think that's deep enough?"

"We-ell, lads, each of you do six more shovelfuls and we'll call it a day. But if we don't get it right now, I'll have trouble later. Get it right and I can rest easy till Judgment Day."

"Won't we be seeing you any more after this, George?"

"Today and tonight. Then I'm going to be leaving for good, Joey, me lad. No sense hanging around when things are the way they ought to be. When everything is settled up and there are no loose ends, a man can rest. If his conscience is clear, of course."

"Does that really make a difference?" asked Pete.

"Does it! I could tell you stories about friends of mine who will *never* get straightened out, because of the things they can't forget, things that weigh on their minds and will for all eternity."

"You wouldn't want to tell us, would you, George? We got nothing much to do today, have we, Pete?"

"Not a thing, Joe, and this is our last chance, George. If we do ten shovels apiece deeper, instead of six, would you tell us?"

"You boys get them bones buried right as rain and I'll have some time for you. We could go up by the old

E

"Get it right, and I can rest easy till Judgement Day!"

light and watch the river, so's I can always have the look of it in my mind. Don't know as I could spend a better day."

The boys did twenty shovels apiece till they were shoulder deep. Then they put some pine boughs in the bottom of the grave and laid the bones out, more or less the way they ought to have lain, only snugger. There were a lot of odds and ends they couldn't recognise, but they put the head at the top, and the arms along the sides, the ribs in the middle, then the legs. The odds and ends they laid neatly in the centre. George's voice kept saying how pleased he was, and how grateful. Then they put some more pine boughs over the lot of them and began the filling in.

"Do you need any words said, George?" asked Joe.

"Well, now, boy, that's real nice of you to remember. I reckon it would make it more official and there sure weren't any words said last time, only a few cuss words. You might each think a little prayer or something."

"Does it matter what kind, George? I'm Catholic and Pete here is some kind of Protestant——"

"Presbyterian," corrected Pete.

"You fellers each say one of your own kind and that'll do fine. I didn't get around to go to much of any church in the old days, so the brand won't matter. You might say 'em silent-like. That'll do first rate."

So the boys said a prayer apiece and when they raised their heads they looked over to the place where the voice had been coming from. Only now George was standing there again and his face was one great smile. "That sure was mighty right and nice."

After that it didn't take them very long to finish the job. They were agreed that it would be better not to put any stones or marker over the spot, since, in the summertime, the Staats family came back once in a while to the burying ground and they might wonder about a new grave. Instead they pulled some vines over the place and piled up some leaves that were blown into a corner. Then they stood back a way and found that they had done a good job of concealment.

"Let's go ask my mother for some sandwiches and tell her we're going up to the other end of the island to explore. Will you come, George?"

"Today I'll do whatever you lads want me to."

"We want to hear about your friends, the ones who can't rest on account of their consciences," Pete said.

THE LADS WHO MET THE HIGHWAYMAN

By SORCHE NIC LEODHAS

THERE WAS a barrister lived in Edinburgh who was so matter-of-fact and dry as dust that a body'd never have believed that anything out of the way could ever have happened to him. But one night when he was sitting in company after dinner, and talk began to go around about strange things they'd heard, one of the men at the table remarked that it was queer that nobody ever heard such a tale from the person directly concerned in it but always at second-hand or even third-hand.

The barrister spoke up at that and said that there was one experience that he could tell them at first-hand. He could vouch for the truth of it himself, because it happened to him and one of his brothers when they were lads still going to school.

His age at the time was about fourteen and his brother was a year younger. As lads will at that age, they were beginning to feel that they were old enough to do a bit of planning for themselves. The summer holidays when they'd be out of school were close at hand, so they decided they'd like to take a trip somewhere together just to do and see something different for a change. Barring a trip or two to the seashore when they were very small, they'd never been far from Edinburgh. Like many Scottish folk, their parents had acquired a good-sized family and little money to tinkle in their pockets, as time went on. So most of their pleasures were home-made and their outings were seldom farther than their legs would carry them. When there are half a dozen lads and a couple of lasses in a family to feed and clothe and give an education, there's never any money left to pay for junketing away from home for holidays.

The father of the lads had a younger brother who had a good-sized croft in the Highlands. The lads had never seen the croft, and they thought it would be a grand plan to go and visit this uncle until school took up again. They had it all worked out well beforehand. So when they got out of school and were back home they went and asked their father if they could.

"You'll not need to be laying out a penny for us," the older lad told him proudly. "We've been saving all year from our pocket money and we have plenty to pay both our fares, up and back again."

"Besides," the younger brother put in, "you'll be in pocket whatever you'd have laid out for our keep while we were at home. You'll save that clear, if we go."

It amused their father quite a bit to find them so businesslike, but he kept a straight face and treated the matter seriously.

"I can't see that I'll be saving anything at all," he objected. "I'll have to be paying your uncle for your keep."

"You'll not have to be doing that," the lads assured him, "for we'll be working on the croft for our keep."

Their father saw that they had it well thought out. It did not sound unreasonable, though he was not sure how much their work would be worth to their uncle. He told them he was willing for them to go providing that their uncle was willing for them to come.

So they wrote and told their uncle that if he'd let them come and stay until school took up again, they'd earn their keep at whatever work he set them to do.

Their uncle wrote back that they might come as soon as they pleased and stay as long as they liked. He'd be glad to have a couple of pairs of extra hands to help him. So the whole family got to work getting their clothes ready and packing them up, and off the two lads went to the croft in the Highlands.

Being town-bred they had plenty to learn and were kept busy. But they learned quick and, as they were willing and neither lad was lazy, before very long they proved to be of real use to their uncle. They liked their aunt and their uncle and were liked in return. On the whole, the life suited them. They were glad they had come.

Their uncle particularly enjoyed having them about. He had no bairns of his own and he regretted it sorely. So he treated the lads as if they had been his own sons, taking care that they were not idle yet not working them too hard, and making sure that they had a reasonable amount of free time for themselves. He was still young enough to remember what it was like to be a lad, so he put them in the way of having any sort of enjoyment that could be had.

One day their uncle's shepherd told them there were going to be some dog trials at the market town six miles away on the coming Saturday. They'd heard often about dog trials, but had never had an opportunity to see any; so they set their hearts on going as soon as the shepherd told them. They went to their uncle and asked his leave to be off from their work on Saturday so that they could walk over to the town to see the dogs at work.

"Och!" said their uncle thumping his head with his fist. "And me for a dumb ox! I meant to tell you we'd be going on Saturday but I forgot. There's no need for you to be walking. We'll go in the cart." So early on the Saturday the lads and their uncle went off to town.

It was a wonderful day for the lads. They'd never have believed that dogs could be so knowing. The way they rounded the sheep up, turning them this way and that way, and sending them wherever they ought to go with no more sign from the shepherd than a lifted finger or maybe a nod of the head was amazing. The dog that belonged to their uncle's shepherd came off with a prize which made the lads almost burst with the pride of it. When all was over they came back from the field to the town fair blazing with excitement.

As they reached the edge of the town they saw that a fair had pitched its booths there. At once the lads were at their uncle. Could they not just go and have a look at the fair? After such a grand day the fair would be the best sort of end to it.

Their uncle shook his head. He must get back to the croft. The men would see to things, no doubt, but he must go about the place to make sure naught was left undone. He could not wait for them to carry them back in the cart, he told them.

"We weren't expecting it," they told him. "We'll not mind walking."

Their uncle regarded them doubtfully for a while, but then said, "Och, ye'll be taking no harm from it." He put his hand in his pocket and drew out his purse.

"I doubt you'll be leaving the fair till the last booth's taken down and folded away. So mind this!" he said as he gave them some money. "I'll not have you travelling on the Sabbath Day. If you find you've not left enough time to get back home well before midnight, you'll have to stay until Monday in the hotel. And have a care that you attend the kirk here morning and evening, should you stay!"

Before they could thank him properly he had rattled off in the cart. They had a bit of money of their own, for their father had sent them their pocket money, just as he always did when they were at school. So they put the money their uncle had given them in the older lad's purse and he put it carefully away in an inside pocket so as to be sure it was extra safe. Then they crossed the field and came up to the fair.

It was none so big but it had most of the usual things you find in fairs. There was a roundabout and a giant swing and a small switchback to ride upon. There were half a dozen booths with freaks and tumblers and the like, and a coconut shy. But it pleased the lads anyway. Still, a fair like that does not take long for one to tire of it. After they'd made the rounds of it several times the lads were ready to leave. They went into the town and found the hotel. But what with the folks who had come for the dog trials, staying so as not to travel on the Sunday, and those who were in the town on other business, there was no room left for the lads. It was only half an hour after nine and still not dark. Six miles does not seem so long when you are at the beginning of it, so the two of them decided to start to walk back to the croft. They were both used to walking and they'd get there well before midnight.

The first couple of miles they went along larking about as lads will do and playing tricks on each other. The excitement of the day had not worn off and they were pleased at the thought of giving back to their uncle the money he'd given them for the hotel. But before they were more than half way back night had fallen. They began to feel the length of the road they must still cover. The croft seemed a far way off. So they settled down to a steady jog and just trudged along. After a long while they came to the kirk where they'd be going with their aunt and uncle in the morning. Their hearts lightened then, for there was only a little better than a mile left to travel. They were pretty sure there'd be a bit of supper kept back for them, just in case they came in, and it would be welcome. But what would be even more welcome was their bed. Losh! How tired they were! They agreed, talking it over, that the day had been too much for them.

"I don't feel able for the hill," said the elder lad.

"Nor I," sighed the younger.

Just beyond the kirk was a crossroad where the road from Edinburgh crossed the side road they were travelling by. The high road was a good hard road and once there had been a lot of going back and forth on it, what with the mail coach and the stage coach and a sluagh of grand folks in their carriages, but the railway had long ago put an end to all that. Under the moon the road lay empty now at either side, and their own road lay as empty before them. They started across the highway to take the road up the hill that led to their journey's end. They were halfway over before they noticed that there was something big and dark under the great oak tree at the right on the far corner of the roads. Maybe a tinker's van or a broken-down cart, they thought, not caring very much because of the weariness in them. But when they got closer they saw that it was a huge black horse. The horse was so dark that it was almost hidden in the shadow under the tree. Then they saw that it bore a man upon its back. The man was as dark as the horse, for he wore a long black cloak and a soft wide-brimmed hat as black as the cloak and the horse. The lads both thought it was a strange-looking pair to be meeting in that place at that hour, but they gave him a polite "Good e'en" and made to pass by on their way. Then they stopped dead in their tracks. In answer to their greeting the man brought both his hands up from under his cloak and in each hand was a long black pistol. The lads stood stock-still, too terrified to move. The pistols were the old-fashioned kind that were seldom seen nowadays, but they had a terribly businesslike look to them. Then the man spoke, in a quiet, easy voice that was as frightening as the pistols. "I'll have what money you've got, my friends," said the man, "and look sharp about it!"

All the money the lads had left was what they were carrying back to their uncle, but they didn't stop to argue with the man. The older lad made haste to pull his purse from his pocket and he hurled it with all his might at the dark stranger. The man caught it deftly but the lads did not wait to find out if he was satisfied with the contents. The two of them took to their heels and fairly flew up the hill. The wind itself would have been put to it to keep up with them. They ran till they reached their uncle's house and burst through the doorway and tumbled over each other into the room where their uncle and aunt were sitting, having a quiet cup of tea before going off to bed.

Their uncle set down his cup with a crash and jumped up from his chair. "What's amiss with you, lads?" he cried in alarm.

"We've been robbed!" cried the older lad, getting his breath at last.

"It was a man all in black on a big black horse,"

panted the younger lad. "He was down by the oak at the crossroads."

"He held a pair of pistols on us and asked for our money. We were bringing what you gave us back to you, but I just pitched the purse at him and then we ran. 'Tis a shame we lost if for you," the older lad said regretfully.

"Maybe he'll be coming after us," his brother said fearfully.

Their uncle stared at them for a minute. Then he burst into a roar of laughter. He sat down in his chair again and took up his cup of tea. "Och!" he told them. "'Tis plain to see that you've been getting acquainted with the ghost of our highwayman!"

"Ghost!" the lads exclaimed.

"Aye," said their uncle. "I've ne'er seen the fellow myself, but I know many a one that has. He'd ne'er do you any harm."

"But he looked so real," the lads protested.

"He has not been real for a hundred years or more," the uncle told them. "Och, he was a slippery one. They were hard put to lay hands on him. But they nabbed him at last. It turned out that he was a well respected gentleman from the town. He'd always been a decent-seeming quiet sort of a body with plenty of money. It gave them a turn when they found where he was getting it from. They caught him there at the crossroads and, after he'd been tried at the assizes, they brought him back and hanged him there where they caught him. He's buried there, too. 'Twas the custom in those days. You could have kept your purse in your pocket and walked right past him He'd not have harmed you at all."

"But he has the money," insisted the older lad. "He caught the purse in his hand."

"Maybe so," said his uncle. "Come now! Eat up your piece and drink your tea. 'Tis close on midnight. By the looks of you, you're needing your sleep the night."

Well, when they walked down to kirk next morn, there was the purse in the grass under the oak tree at the crossroads. Their uncle picked it up and handed it to them. "Your highwayman had no need for your money," he said with a smile. "You'd best keep it for yourselves. You've earned it."

When they went back to Edinburgh at the end of their holidays they had a grand story to tell all their friends and you may be sure they made the most of it.

It wasn't the last they saw of the croft, for the two brothers went back every summer to lend their uncle a hand. For that matter they still do, for they've taken the place of sons to their uncle and aunt. But although they have travelled up and down the hill a hundred times or more, they have never again met up with the ghost of the highwayman.

A PAIR OF HANDS

By SIR ARTHUR QUILLER-COUCH

"YES," said Miss Le Petyt, gazing into the deep fireplace and letting her hands and her knitting lie idle for the moment in her lap. "Oh, yes, I have seen a ghost. In fact, I have lived in a house with one for quite a long time."

"How could you——" began one of my host's daughters; and "You, Aunt Emily?" cried the other at the same moment.

Miss Le Petyt, gentle soul, withdrew her eyes from the fireplace and protested with a gay little smile. "Well, my dears, I am not quite the coward you take me for. And, as it happens, mine was the most harmless ghost in the world. In fact"—and here she looked at the fire again—"I was quite sorry to lose her."

"It was a woman, then? Now, I think," said Miss Blanche, "that female ghosts are the horridest of all. They wear little shoes with high red heels, and go about tap, tap, wringing their hands."

"This one wrung her hands, certainly. But I don't know about the high red heels, for I never saw her feet. Perhaps she was like the Queen of Spain, and hadn't any. And as for the hands, it all depends how you wring them. There's an elderly shopwalker at Knightsbridge, for instance——"

142

"Don't be prosy, dear, when you know that we're just dying to hear the story."

Miss Le Petyt turned to me with a small deprecating laugh. "It's such a little one."

"The story or the ghost?"

"Both."

And this was Miss Le Petyt's story:

"It happened when I lived down in Cornwall, at Tresillack, on the south coast. Tresillack was the name of the house, which stood quite alone at the head of a coombe, within sound of the sea but without sight of it; for though the coombe led down to a wide open beach it wound and twisted half a dozen times on its way, and its overlapping sides closed the view from the house, which was advertised as 'secluded.' I was very poor in those days. Your father and all of us were poor then, as I trust, my dears, you will never be; but I was young enough to be romantic and wise enough to like independence, and this word 'secluded' took my fancy.

"The misfortune was that it had taken the fancy, or just suited the requirements, of several previous tenants. You know, I dare say, the kind of person who rents a secluded house in the country? Well, yes, there are several kinds; but they seem to agree in being odious. No one knows where they come from, though they soon remove all doubt about where they're 'going to,' as the children say. 'Shady' is the word, is it not? Well, the previous tenants of Tresillack (from first to last a bewildering series) had been shady with a vengeance.

"I knew nothing of this when I first made
143

application to the landlord, a solid yeoman inhabiting a farm at the foot of the coombe, on a cliff overlooking the beach.

"To him I presented myself fearlessly as a spinster of decent family and small but assured income, intending a rural life of combined seemliness and economy. He met my advances politely enough, but with an air of suspicion which offended me. I began by disliking him for it; afterwards I set it down as an unpleasant feature in the local character. I was doubly mistaken. Farmer Hosking was slow-witted, but as honest a man as ever stood up against hard times; and a more open and hospitable race than the people on that coast I never wish to meet. It was the caution of a child who had burnt his fingers, not once but many times. Had I known what I afterwards learned of Farmer Hosking's tribulations as landlord of a 'secluded country residence,' I should have approached him with the bashfulness proper to my suit and faltered as I undertook to prove the bright exception in a long line of painful experiences. He had bought the Tresillack estate twenty years before—on mortgage, I fancy—because the land adjoined his own and would pay him for tillage. But the house was a nuisance, an incubus; and had been so from the beginning.

" 'Well, miss,' he said, 'you're welcome to look over it; a pretty enough place, inside and out. There's no trouble about keys, because I've put in a housekeeper, a widow-woman, and she'll show you round. With your leave I'll step up the coombe so far with you, and put you in your way.' As I thanked him he paused and rubbed his chin. 'There's one thing I must tell you, though. Whoever takes the house must take Mrs. Carkeek along with it.'

" 'Mrs. Carkeek?' I echoed dolefully. 'Is that the housekeeper?'

" 'Yes; she was wife to my late hind. I'm sorry, miss,' he added, my face telling him no doubt what sort of woman I expected Mrs. Carkeek to be; 'but I had to make it a rule after—after some things had happened. And I dare say you won't find her so bad. Mary Carkeek's a sensible, comfortable woman, and knows the place. She was in service there to Squire Kendall when he sold up and went: her first place it was.'

" 'I may as well see the house, anyhow,' said I dejectedly. So we started to walk up the coombe. The path, which ran beside a little chattering stream, was narrow for the most part, and Farmer Hosking, with an apology, strode on ahead to beat aside the brambles. But whenever its width allowed us to walk side by side I caught him from time to time stealing a shy inquisitive glance under his rough eyebrows. Courteously though he bore himself, it was clear that he could not sum me up to his satisfaction or bring me square with his notion of a tenant of his 'secluded country residence.'

"I don't know what foolish fancy prompted it, but about half-way up the coombe I stopped short and asked:

" 'There are no ghosts, I suppose?'

"It struck me, a moment after I had uttered it, as a supremely silly question; but he took it quite seriously. 'No: I never heard tell of any ghosts.' He laid a queer sort of stress on the word. 'There's always been

145

trouble with servants, and maids' tongues will be runnin'. But Mary Carkeek lives up there alone, and she seems comfortable enough.'

"We walked on. By and by he pointed with his stick. 'It don't look like a place for ghosts, now, do it?'

"Certainly it did not. Above an untrimmed orchard rose a terrace of turf scattered with thorn bushes, and above this a terrace of stone, upon which stood the prettiest cottage I had ever seen. It was long and low and thatched; a deep verandah ran from end to end. Clematis, banksia roses and honeysuckle climbed the posts of this verandah, and big blooms of Marechal Niel were clustered along its roof, beneath the lattices of the bedroom windows. The house was small enough to be called a cottage, and rare enough in features and in situation to confer distinction on any tenant. It suggested what in those days we should have called 'elegant' living. And I could have clapped my hands for joy.

"My spirits mounted still higher when Mrs. Carkeek opened the door to us. I had looked for a Mrs. Gummidge, and I found a healthy middle-aged woman with a thoughtful, but contented, face, and a smile which, without a trace of obsequiousness, quite bore out the farmer's description of her. She was a comfortable woman; and while we walked through the rooms together (for Mr. Hosking waited outside) I 'took to' Mrs. Carkeek. Her speech was direct and practical; the rooms, in spite of their faded furniture, were bright and exquisitely clean; and somehow the very atmosphere of the house gave me a sense of well-being, of feeling at home and cared for; yes, of being loved. Don't laugh, my dears; for when I've done you may not think this fancy altogether foolish.

"I stepped out into the verandah, and Farmer Hosking pocketed the pruning-knife which he had been using on a bush of jasmine.

" 'This is better than anything I had dreamed of,' said I.

" 'Well, miss, that's not a wise way of beginning a bargain, if you'll excuse me.'

"He took no advantage, however, of my admission; and we struck the bargain as we returned down the coombe to his farm, where the hired chaise waited to convey me back to the market town. I had meant to engage a maid of my own, but now it occurred to me that I might do very well with Mrs. Carkeek. This, too, was settled in the course of the next day or two, and within the week I have moved into my new home.

"I can hardly describe to you the happiness of my first month at Tresillack, because (as I now believe) if I take the reasons which I had for being happy, one by one, there remains over something which I cannot account for. I was moderately young, entirely healthy; I felt myself independent and adventurous; the season was high summer, the weather glorious, the garden in all the pomp of June, yet sufficiently unkempt to keep me busy, give me a sharp appetite for meals, and send me to bed in that drowsy stupor which comes of the odours of earth. I spent the most of my time out of doors, winding up the day's work as a rule with a walk down the cool valley, along the beach and back.

"I soon found that all housework could be safely left to Mrs. Carkeek. She did not talk much; indeed, her

147

only fault (a rare one in housekeepers) was that she talked too little, and even when I addressed her seemed at times unable to give me her attention. It was as though her mind strayed off to some small job she had forgotten, and her eyes wore a listening look, as though she waited for the neglected task to speak and remind her. But, as a matter of fact, she forgot nothing. Indeed, my dears, I was never so well attended to in my life.

"Well, that is what I'm coming to. That, so to say, is just it. The woman not only had the rooms swept and dusted and my meals prepared to the moment.

"In a hundred odd little ways this orderliness, these preparations, seemed to read my desires. Did I wish the roses renewed in a bowl upon the dining-table, sure enough at the next meal they would be replaced by fresh ones. Mrs. Carkeek (I told myself) must have surprised and interpreted a glance of mine. And yet I could not remember having glanced at the bowl in her presence. And how on earth had she guessed the very roses, the very shapes and colours I had lightly wished for? This is only an instance, you understand? Every day, and from morning to night, I happened on others, each slight enough, but all together bearing witness to a ministering intelligence as subtle as it was untiring.

"I am a light sleeper, as you know, with an uncomfortable knack of waking with the sun and roaming early. No matter how early I rose at Tresillack, Mrs. Carkeek seemed to have preceded me. Finally I had to conclude that she arose and dusted and tidied as soon as she judged me safely a-bed. For once, finding the drawing-room (where I had been sitting late) 'redded up' at four in the morning, and no trace of a plate of raspberries which I had carried thither after dinner and left overnight, I determined to test her, and walked through to the kitchen, calling her by name.

"I found the kitchen as clean as a pin, and the fire laid, but no trace of Mrs. Carkeek. I walked upstairs and knocked at her door. At the second knock, a sleepy voice cried out, and presently the good woman stood before me in her nightgown, looking (I thought) very badly scared.

" 'No,' I said, 'it's not a burglar. But I've found out what I wanted, that you do your morning's work overnight. But you mustn't wait for me when I choose to sit up. And now go back to your bed like a good soul, whilst I take a run down to the beach.'

"She stood blinking in the dawn. Her face was still white.

" 'O, miss,' she gasped, 'I made sure you must have seen something!'

" 'And so I have,' I answered, 'but it was neither burglars nor ghosts.'

" 'Thank God!' I heard her say as she turned her back to me in her grey bedroom—which faced the north. And I took this for a carelessly pious expression and ran downstairs thinking no more of it.

"A few days later I began to understand.

"The plan of Tresillack house (I must explain) was simplicity itself. To the left of the hall as you entered was the dining-room; to the right the drawing-room, with a boudoir beyond. The foot of the stairs faced the front door, and beside it, passing a glazed inner door, you found two others right and left, the left opening on

149

the kitchen, the right on a passage which ran by a store cupboard under the bend of the stairs to a neat pantry with the usual shelves and linen-press, and under the window (which faced north) a porcelain basin and brass tap. On the first morning of my tenancy I had visited this pantry and turned the tap, but no water ran. I supposed this to be accidental. Mrs. Carkeek had to wash up glass ware and crockery, and no doubt Mrs. Carkeek would complain of any failure in the water supply.

"But the day after my surprise visit (as I called it) I had picked a basketful of roses, and carried them into the pantry as a handy place to arrange them in. I chose a china bowl and went to fill it at the tap. Again the water would not run.

"I called Mrs. Carkeek. 'What is wrong with this tap?' I asked. 'The rest of the house is well enough supplied.'

" 'I don't know, miss. I never use it.'

" 'But there must be a reason; and you must find it a great nuisance washing up the plates and glasses in the kitchen. Come around to the back with me, and we'll have a look at the cisterns.'

" 'The cisterns'll be all right, miss. I assure you I don't find it a trouble.'

"But I was not to be put off. The back of the house stood but ten feet from a wall which was really but a stone face built against the cliff cut away by the architect. Above the cliff rose the kitchen garden, and from its lower path we looked over the wall's parapet upon the cisterns. There were two—a very large one,

150

supplying the kitchen and the bathroom above the kitchen; and a small one, obviously fed by the other, and as obviously leading by a pipe which I could trace, to the pantry. Now the big cistern stood almost full, and yet the small one, though on a lower level was empty.

" 'It's as plain as daylight,' said I. 'The pipe between the two is choked.' And I clambered on to the parapet.

" 'I wouldn't, miss. The pantry tap is only cold water, and no use to me. From the kitchen boiler I get it hot, you see.'

" 'But I want the pantry water for my flowers.' I bent over and groped. 'I thought as much!' said I, as I wrenched out a thick plug of cork, and immediately the water began to flow. I turned triumphantly on Mrs. Carkeek, who had grown suddenly red in the face. Her eyes were fixed on the cork in my hand. To keep it more firmly wedged in its place somebody had wrapped it round with a rag of calico print; and discoloured though the rag was, I seemed to recall the pattern (a lilac sprig). Then, as our eyes met, it occurred to me that only two mornings before Mrs. Carkeek had worn a print gown of that same sprigged pattern.

"I had the presence of mind to hide this very small discovery, sliding over it some quite trivial remark; and presently Mrs. Carkeek regained her composure. But I own I felt disappointed in her. It seemed such a paltry thing to be disingenuous over. She had deliberately acted a fib before me; and why? Merely because she preferred the kitchen to the pantry tap. It was childish. 'But servants are all the same,' I told myself. 'I must

151

take Mrs. Carkeek as she is; and, after all, she is a treasure.'

"On the second night after this, and between eleven and twelve o'clock, I was lying in bed and reading myself sleepy over a novel of Lord Lytton's, when a small sound disturbed me. I listened. The sound was clearly that of water trickling, and I set it down to rain. A shower (I told myself) had filled the water-pipes which drained the roof. Somehow I could not fix the sound. There was a water pipe against the wall just outside my window. I rose and drew up the blind.

"To my astonishment no rain was falling; no rain had fallen. I felt the slate window-sill; some dew had gathered there—no more. There was no wind, no cloud; only a still moon high over the eastern slope of the coombe, the distant splash of waves, and the fragrance of many roses. I went back to bed and listened again. Yes, the trickling sound continued, quite distinct in the silence of the house, not to be confused for a moment with the dull murmur of the beach. After a while it began to grate on my nerves. I caught up my candle, flung my dressing-gown about me, and stole softly downstairs.

"Then it was simple. I traced the sound to the pantry. 'Mrs. Carkeek has left the tap running,' said I: and, sure I found it so—a thin trickle steadily running to waste in the porcelain basin. I turned off the tap, went contentedly back to my bed, and slept—

"—for some hours. I opened my eyes in darkness and at once knew what had awakened me. The tap was running again. Now, it had shut easily in my hand, but not so easily that I could believe it had slipped

152

open again of its own accord. 'This is Mrs. Carkeek's doing,' said I; and I am afraid I added 'Drat Mrs. Carkeek!'

"Well there was no help for it: so I struck a light, looked at my watch, saw that the hour was just three o'clock, and I descended the stairs again. At the pantry door I paused. I was not afraid—not one little bit. In fact the notion that anything might be wrong had never crosed my mind. But I remember thinking, with my hand on the door, that if Mrs. Carkeek were in the pantry I might happen to give her a severe fright.

"I pushed the door open briskly. Mrs. Carkeek was not there. But something was there, by the porcelain basin—something which might have sent me scurrying upstairs two steps at a time, but which as a matter of fact held me to the spot. My heart seemed to stand still —so still! And in the stillness I remember setting down the brass candlestick on a tall nest of drawers beside me.

"Over the porcelain basin and beneath the water trickling from the tap I saw two hands.

"That was all—two small hands, a child's hands. I cannot tell how they ended.

"No; they were not cut off. I saw them quite distinctly; just a pair of small hands and the wrists, and after that—nothing. They were moving briskly— washing themselves clean. I saw the water trickle and splash over them—not through them—but just as it would on real hands. They were the hands of a little girl, too. Oh, yes, I was sure of that at once. Boys and girls wash their hands differently. I can't just tell you what the difference is, but it's unmistakable.

"I saw all this before my candle slipped and fell with a crash. I had set it down without looking—for my eyes were fixed on the basin—and had balanced it on the edge of the nest of drawers. After the crash, in the darkness there, with the water running, I suffered some bad moments.

"Oddly enough, the thought uppermost with me was that I must shut off that tap before escaping. I had to. And after a while I picked up all my courage, so to say, between my teeth, and with a little sob thrust out my hand and did it. Then I fled.

"The dawn was close upon me: and as soon as the sky reddened I took my bath, dressed and went downstairs. And there at the pantry door I found Mrs. Carkeek, also dressed, with my candlestick in her hand.

" 'Ah;' said I, 'you picked it up.'

"Our eyes met. Clearly Mrs. Carkeek wished me to begin, and I determined at once to have it out with her.

" 'And you knew all about it. That's what accounts for your plugging up the cistern.'

" 'You saw . . . ?' she began.

" 'Yes, yes. And you must tell me all about it—never mind how bad. Is—is it—murder?'

" 'Law bless you, miss, whatever put such horrors in your head?'

" 'She was washing her hands.'

" 'Ah, so she does, poor dear! But—murder! And dear little Miss Margaret, that wouldn't go to hurt a fly!'

" 'Miss Margaret?'

" 'Eh, she died at seven year. Squire Kendall's only daughter; and that's over twenty years ago. I was her nurse, miss, and I know—diphtheria it was; she took it down in the village.'

" 'But how do you know it is Margaret?'

" 'Those hands—why, how could I mistake, that used to be her nurse?'

" 'But why does she wash them?'

" 'Well, miss, being always a dainty child—and the housework, you see——'

"I took a long breath. 'Do you mean to tell me that all this tidying and dusting——' I broke off. 'Is it she who has been taking this care of me?'

"Mrs. Carkeek met my look steadily.

" 'Who else, miss?'

" 'Poor little soul!'

" 'Well now'—Mrs. Carkeek rubbed my candlestick with the edge of her apron—'I'm so glad you take it like this. For there isn't really nothing to be afraid of —is there?' She eyed me wistfully. 'It's my belief she loves you, miss. But only to think what a time she must have had with the others!'

" 'Were they bad?'

" 'They was awful. Didn't Farmer Hosking tell you? They carried on fearful—one after another, and each one worse than the last.'

" 'What was the matter with them? Drink?'

" 'Drink, miss, with some of 'em. There was the Major—he used to go mad with it, and run about the coombe in his nightshirt. Oh, scandalous! And his wife drank too—that is, if she ever was his wife. Just think of that tender child washing up after their nasty doings!

" 'But that wasn't the worst, miss—not by a long

155

way. There was a pair here—from the colonies, or so they gave out—with two children, a boy and gel, the eldest scarce six. Poor mites!

" 'They beat those children, miss—your blood would boil! And starved, and tortured 'em, it's my belief. You could hear their screams, I've been told, away back in the high-road, and that's the best part of half a mile.

" 'Sometimes they was locked up without food for days together. But it's my belief that little Miss Margaret managed to feed them somehow. Oh, I can see her creeping to the door and comforting!'

" 'But perhaps she never showed herself when these awful people were here, but took to flight until they left.'

" 'You didn't never know her, miss. The brave she was! She'd have stood up to lions. She've been here all the while: and only to think what her innocent eyes and ears must have took in! There was another couple ——" Mrs. Carkeek sunk her voice.

" 'Oh, hush!' said I, 'if I'm to have any peace of mind in this house!'

" 'But you won't go, miss? She loves you, I know she do. And think what you might be leaving her to— what sort of tenant might come next. For she can't go. She've been here ever since her father sold the place. He died soon after. You mustn't go!'

"Now I had resolved to go, but all of a sudden I felt how mean this resolution was.

" 'After all,' said I, 'there's nothing to be afraid of.'

" 'That's it, miss; nothing at all. I don't even believe it's so very uncommon. Why, I've heard my mother

156

tell of farmhouses where the rooms were swept every night as regular as clockwork, and the floors sanded, and the pots and pans scoured, and all while the maids slept. They put it down to the piskies; but we know better, miss, and now we've got the secret between us we can lie easy in our beds, and if we hear anything, say, "God bless the child!" and go to sleep.'

"I spent three years at Tresillack, and all that while Mrs. Carkeek lived with me and shared the secret. Few women, I dare to say, were ever so completely wrapped around with love as we were during those three years.

"It ran through my waking life like a song: it smoothed my pillow, touched and made my table comely, in summer lifted the heads of the flowers as I passed, and in winter watched the fire with me and kept it bright.

" 'Why did I ever leave Tresillack?' Because one day, at the end of five years, Farmer Hosking brought me word that he had sold the house—or was about to sell it; I forget which. There was no avoiding it, at any rate; the purchaser being a Colonel Kendall, a brother of the old Squire.

" 'A married man?' I asked.

" 'Yes, miss; with a family of eight. As pretty children as ever you see, and the mother a good lady. It's the old home to Colonel Kendall.'

" 'I see. And that is why you feel bound to sell.'

" 'It's a good price, too, that he offers. You mustn't think but I'm sorry enough——'

" 'To turn me out? I thank you, Mr. Hosking; but you are doing the right thing.'

157

" 'She—Margaret—will be happy,' I said; 'with her cousins, you know.'

" 'Oh, yes, miss, she will be happy, sure enough,' Mrs. Carkeek agreed.

"So when the time came I packed up my boxes and tried to be cheerful. But on the last morning, when they stood corded in the hall, I sent Mrs. Carkeek upstairs upon some poor excuse, and stepped alone into the pantry.

" 'Margaret!' I whispered.

"There was no answer at all. I had scarcely dared to hope for one. Yet I tried again, and, shutting my eyes this time, stretched out both hands and whispered:

" 'Margaret!'

"And I will swear to my dying day that two little hands stole and rested—for a moment only—in mine."

ACKNOWLEDGEMENTS

The editor gratefully acknowledges permission to reprint copyright material to the following:

Sorche Nic Leodhas and The Bodley Head for SANDY MacNEIL AND HIS DOG, THE GIANT BONES and THE LADS WHO MET THE HIGHWAYMAN.

Manly Wade Wellman and The Garden City Publishing Co. Inc. for SCHOOL FOR THE UNSPEAKABLE.

Edward L. White and Brandt & Brandt for THE HOUSE OF THE NIGHTMARE.

The Executors of the late H. G. Wells and Messrs. A. P. Watt & Son for THE STORY OF THE INEXPERIENCED GHOST and THE RED ROOM.

Halina Gorska and Roy Publishers Inc. for PRINCE GODFREY FREES MOUNTAIN DWELLERS.

The Estate of John Kendrick Bangs and Harper & Row Publishers Inc. for THE WATER GHOST OF HARROWBY HALL.

Louis C. Jones and Houghton Mifflin Co. for SPOOKS OF THE VALLEY.

J. M. Dent & Sons for A PAIR OF HANDS.

COMING IN ARMADA

DECEMBER 1970

3rd Armada Ghost Book

Edited by

MARY DANBY

Price 3s. 6d.